THE
WORLD'S
ONE HUNDRED
BEST SHORT STORIES

[IN TEN VOLUMES]

GRANT OVERTON
EDITOR - IN - CHIEF

VOLUME EIGHT
MEN

FUNK & WAGNALLS COMPANY
NEW YORK AND LONDON

CONTENTS

THE WORLD'S 100 BEST SHORT STORIES

WORDS AND MUSIC

By Irvin S. Cobb

When Breck Tandy killed a man he made a number of mistakes. In the first place, he killed the most popular man in Forked Deer County—the county clerk, a man named Abner J. Rankin. In the second place, he killed him with no witnesses present, so that it stood his word—and he a newcomer and a stranger—against the mute, eloquent accusation of a riddled dead man. And in the third place, he sent north of the Ohio River for a lawyer to defend him.

* * * * * * * * * *

On the first Monday in June—Court Monday—the town filled up early. Before the field larks were out of the grass the farmers were tying their teams to the gnawed hick-racks along the square. By nine o'clock the swapping ring below the wagonyard was swimming in red dust and clamorous with the chaffer of the horse-traders. In front of a vacant store the Ladies' Aid Society of Zion Baptist Church had a canvas sign out, announcing that an elegant dinner would be served for twenty-five cents from twelve to one, also ice cream and cake all day for fifteen cents.

The narrow wooden sidewalks began to creak and churn under the tread of many feet. A long-haired medicine doctor emerged from his frock-coat like a locust coming out of its shell, pushed his high hat off his forehead and ranged a guitar, sundry bottles of a potent mixture, his tooth-pulling forceps, and a trick-handkerchief upon the narrow shelf of his stand alongside the Drummers' Home Hotel. In front of the little dingy tent of the Half Man and Half Horse a yellow negro sat on a split-bottom chair limbering up for a hard day. This yellow negro was an artist. He played a common twenty-cent mouth organ, using his left hand to slide it back and forth across his spread lips. The other hand held a pair of polished beef bones, such as end men wield, and about the wrist was buckled a broad leather strap with three big sleigh-bells riveted loosely to the leather, so that he could clap the bones and shake the bells with the same motion. He was a whole orchestra in himself. He could play on his mouth organ almost any tune you wanted, and with his bones and his bells to help out he could creditably imitate a church organ, a fife-and-drum corps, or, indeed, a full brass band. He had his chair tilted back until his woolly head dented a draggled banner depicting in five faded primary colors the physical attractions of the Half Man and Half Horse—Marvel of the Century—and he tested his mouth organ with short, mellow, tentative blasts as he waited until the Marvel and the Marvel's manager finished a belated breakfast within and the first ballyhoo could start. He was practising the newest of the ragtime airs to get that far South. The name of it was The Georgia Camp-Meeting.

The town marshal in his shirt sleeves, with a big

silver shield pinned to the breast of his unbuttoned
blue waistcoat and hickory stick with a crook handle
for added emblem of authority, stalked the town
drunkard, fair game at all seasons and especially on
Court Monday. The town gallant whirled back and
forth the short hilly length of Main Street in his new
side-bar buggy. A clustering group of negroes made a
thick, black blob, like hiving bees, in front of a negro
fishhouse, from which came the smell and sounds of
perch and channel cat frying on spitting-hot skillets.
High up on the squat cupola of the courthouse a red-
headed woodpecker clung, barred in crimson, white,
and blue-black, like a bit of living bunting, engaged
in the hopeless task of trying to drill through the tin
sheathing. The rolling rattle of his beak's tattoo came
down sharply to the crowd below. Mourning doves
called to one another in the trees round the red-brick
courthouse, and at ten o'clock, when the sun was
high and hot, the sheriff came out and, standing between two hollow white pillars, rapped upon one of
them with a stick and called upon all witnesses and
talesmen to come into court for the trial of John
Breckinridge Tandy, charged with murder in the first
degree, against the peace and dignity of the commonwealth of Tennessee and the statutes made and pro-
vided.

But this ceremonial by the sheriff was for form
rather than effect, since the witnesses and the talesmen
all sat in the circuit-court chamber along with as many
of the population of Forked Deer County as could
squeeze in there. Already the air of the crowded chamber was choky with heat and rancid with smell. Men
were perched precariously in the ledges of the windows. More men were ranged in rows along the

plastered walls, clunking their heels against the cracked wooden baseboards. The two front rows of benches were full of women. For this was to be the big case of the June term—a better show by long odds than the Half Man and Half Horse.

Inside the low railing that divided the room and on the side nearer the jury box were the forces of the defense. Under his skin the prisoner showed a sallow paleness born of his three months in the county jail. He was tall and dark and steady eyed, a young man, well under thirty. He gave no heed to those who sat in packed rows behind him, wishing him evil. He kept his head turned front, only bending it sometimes to whisper with one of his lawyers or one of his witnesses. Frequently, tho, his hand went out in a protecting, reassuring way to touch his wife's brown hair or to rest a moment on her small shoulder. She was a plain, scared, shrinking little thing. The fingers of her thin hand were plaited desperately together in her lap. Already she was trembling. Once in a while she would raise her face, showing shallow brown eyes dilated with fright, and then sink her head again like a quail trying to hide. She looked pitiable and lonely.

The chief attorney for the defense was half turned from the small counsel table where he might study the faces of the crowd. He was from Middle Indiana, serving his second term in Congress. If his party held control of the state he would go to the Senate after the next election. He was an orator of parts and a pleader of almost a national reputation. He had manly grace and he was a fine, upstanding figure of a man, and before now he had wrung victories out of many difficult cases. But he chilled to his finger-nails with apprehensions of disaster as he glanced searchingly about the close-packed room.

Wherever he looked he saw no friendliness at all. He could feel the hostility of that crowd as tho it had substance and body. It was a tangible thing; it was almost a physical thing. Why, you could almost put your hand out and touch it. It was everywhere there.

And it focussed and was summed up in the person of Aunt Tilly Haslett, rearing on the very front bench with her husband, Uncle Fayette, half hidden behind her vast and overflowing bulk. Aunt Tilly made public opinion in Hyattsville. Indeed she was public opinion in that town. In her it had its up-comings and its out-flowings. She held herself bolt upright, filling out the front of her black bombazine basque until the buttons down its front strained at their buttonholes. With wide, deliberate strokes she fanned herself with a palm-leaf fan. The fan had an edging of black tape sewed round it—black tape signifying in that community age or mourning, or both. Her jaw was set like a steel latch, and her little gray eyes behind her steel-bowed specs were leveled with a baleful, condemning glare that included the strange lawyer, his client, his client's wife, and all that was his client's.

Congressman Durham looked and knew that his presence was an affront to Aunt Tilly and all those who sat with her; that his somewhat vivid tie, his silken shirt, his low tan shoes, his new suit of gray flannels—a masterpiece of the best tailor in Indianapolis—were as insults, added up and piled on, to this suspendered, gingham-shirted constituency. Better than ever he realized now the stark hopelessness of the task to which his hands were set. And he dreaded what was coming almost as much for himself as for the man he was hired to defend. But he was a trained veteran of courtroom campaigns, and there was a jauntily assumed confidence in his bearing as he swung himself about and made a brisk show of conferring with the local attorney who was to aid him in the choosing of the jurors and the questioning of the witnesses.

But it was real confidence and real jauntiness that radiated from the other wing of the inclosure, where the prosecutor sat with the assembled bar of Forked Deer County on his flanks, volunteers upon the favored side, lending to it the moral support of weight and numbers. Rankin, the dead man, having been a bachelor, State's Attorney Gilliam could bring no lorn widow and children to mourn before the jurors' eyes and win added sympathy for his cause. Lacking these most valued assets of a murder trial he supplied their places with the sisters of the dead man—two sparse-built elderly women in heavy black, with sweltering thick veils down over their faces. When the proper time came he would have them raise these veils and show their woeful faces, but now they sat shrouded all in crepe, fit figures of desolation and sorrow. He fussed about busily, fiddling the quill toothpick that hung perilously in the corner of his mouth and evening up the edges of a pile of law books with freckled calfskin covers. He was a lank, bony garfish of a man, with a white goatee aggressively protruding from his lower lip. He was a poor speaker but mighty as a cross-examiner, and he was serving his first term and was a candidate for another. He wore the official garbing of special and extraordinary occasions—long black coat and limp white waistcoat and gray striped trousers, a trifle short in the legs.

He felt the importance of his place here almost visibly—his figure swelled and expanded out his clothes.

"Look yonder at Tom Gilliam," said Mr. Lukins, the grocer, in tones of whispered admiration to his next-elbow neighbor, "jest prunin' and honin' hisse'f to git at that there Tandy and his dude Yankee lawyer. If he don't chaw both of 'em up together I'll be dadburned."

"You bet," whispered back his neighbor—it was Aunt Tilly's oldest son, Fayette, Junior—"it's like Maw says—time's come to teach them murderin' Kintuckians they can't be a-comin' down here a-killin' up people and not pay for it. I reckon, Mr. Lukins," added Fayette, Junior, with a wriggle of pleased anticipation, "we shore are goin' to see some carryin's-on in this cotehouse today."

Mr. Lukins' reply was lost to history because just then the judge entered—an elderly, kindly-looking man—from his chambers in the rear, with the circuitcourt clerk right behind him bearing large leather-clad books and sheaves of foolscap paper. Their coming made a bustle. Aunt Tilly squared herself forward, scrooging Uncle Fayette yet farther into the eclipse of her shapeless figure. The prisoner raised his head and eyed his judge. His wife looked only at the interlaced, weaving fingers in her lap.

The formalities of the opening of a term of court were mighty soon over; there was everywhere manifest a haste to get at the big thing. The clerk called the case of the Commonwealth versus Tandy. Both sides were ready. Through the local lawyer, delegated for these smaller purposes, the accused man pleaded not guilty. The clerk spun the jury wheel, which was a painted wooden drum on a creaking wooden axle, and

drew forth a slip of paper with the name of a talesman
written upon it and read aloud:

"Isom W. Tolliver."

In an hour the jury was complete: two townsmen,
a clerk and a telegraph operator, and ten men from the
country—farmers mainly and one blacksmith and one
horse-trader. Three of the panel who owned up frankly
to a fixed bias had been let go by consent of both sides.
Three more were sure they could give the defendant a
fair trial, but those three the local lawyer had chal-
lenged peremptorily. The others were accepted as they
came. The foreman was a brownskinned, sparrow-
hawk-looking old man, with a smoldering brown eye.
He had spare, knotted hands, like talons, and the right
one was marred and twisted, with a sprayed bluish
scar in the midst of the crippled knuckles like the mark
of an old gunshot wound. Juror No. 4 was a stodgy
old man, a small planter from the back part of the
county, who fanned himself steadily with a brown-
varnished straw hat. No. 7 was even older, a white-
whiskered patriarch on crutches. The twelfth juryman was the oldest of the twelve—he looked to be
almost seventy, but he went into the box after he had
sworn that his sight and hearing and general health
were good and that he still could do his ten hours a
day at his blacksmith shop. This juryman chewed
tobacco without pause. Twice after he took his seat
at the back end of the double line he tried for a
wooden cuspidor ten feet away. Both were creditable
attempts, but he missed each time. Seeing the look
of gathering distress in his eyes the sheriff brought the
cuspidor nearer, and thereafter No. 12 was content,
chewing steadily like some bearded contemplative
ruminant and listening attentively to the evidence.

meanwhile scratching a very wiry head of white-red hair with a thumbnail that through some injury had taken on the appearance of a very thick, very black Brazil nut. This scratching made a raspy, filing sound that after a while got on Congressman Durham's nerves.

It was late in the afternoon when the prosecution rested its case and court adjourned until the following morning. The state's attorney had not had so very much evidence to offer, really—the testimony of one who heard the single shot and ran in at Rankin's door to find Rankin upon the floor, about dead, with a pistol, unfired, in his hand and Tandy standing against the wall with a pistol, fired, in his hand; the constable to whom Tandy surrendered; the physician who examined the body; the persons who knew of the quarrel between Tandy and Rankin growing out of a land deal into which they had gone partners—not much, but enough for Gilliam's purposes. Once in the midst of examining a witness the state's attorney, seemingly by accident, let his look fall upon the two black-robed. silent figures at his side, and as tho overcome by the sudden realization of a great grief, he faltered and stopped dead and sank down. It was an old trick, but well done, and a little humming murmur like a breeze coming through treetops swept the audience.

Durham was sick in his soul as he came away. In his mind there stood the picture of a little, scared woman's drawn, drenched face. She had started crying before the last juror was chosen and thereafter all day, at half-minute intervals, the big, hard sobs racked her. As Durham came down the steps he had almost to shove his way through a knot of natives outside the

doors. They grudged him the path they made for
him, and as he showed them his back he heard a snicker
and some one said a thing that cut him where he was
already bruised—in his egotism. But he gave no heed
to the words. What was the use?

At the Drummers' Home Hotel a darky waiter sus-
tained a profound shock when the imported lawyer de-
clined the fried beefsteak with fried potatoes and also
the fried ham and eggs. Mastering his surprize the
waiter offered to try to get the Northern gentleman
a fried pork chop and some fried June apples, but
Durham only wanted a glass of milk for his supper.
He drank it and smoked a cigar, and about dusk he
went upstairs to his room. There he found assembled the forlorn rank and file of the defense, the local
lawyer and three character witnesses—prominent cit-
izens from Tandy's home town who were to testify
to his good repute in the place where he was born and
reared. These would be the only witnesses, except
Tandy himself, that Durham meant to call. One of
them was a bustling little man named Felsburg, a
clothing merchant, and one was Colonel Quigley, a
banker and an ex-mayor, and the third was a Judge
Priest, who sat on a circuit-court bench back in Ken-
tucky. In contrast to his size, which was considerable,
this Judge Priest had a voice that was high and whiny.
He also had the trick, common to many men in politics
in his part of the South, of being purposely ungram-
matical at times.

This mannerism led a lot of people into thinking that
the judge must be an uneducated man—until they
heard him charging a jury or reading one of his rulings.
The judge had other peculiarities. In conversation
he nearly always called men younger than himself, son.

He drank a little bit too much sometimes; and nobody had ever beaten him for any office he coveted. Durham didn't know what to make of this old judge—sometimes he seemed simple-minded to the point of childishness almost.

The others were gathered about a table by a lighted kerosene lamp, but the old judge sat at an open window with his low-quarter shoes off and his white-socked feet propped against the ledge. He was industriously stoking at a home-made corncob pipe. He pursed up his mouth, pulling at the long cane stem of his pipe with little audible sucks. From the rocky little street below the clatter of departing farm teams came up to him. The Indian medicine doctor was taking down his big white umbrella and packing up his regalia. The late canvas habitat of the Half Man and Half Horse had been struck and was gone, leaving only the pole-holes in the turf and a trodden space to show where it had stood. Court would go on all week, but Court Monday was over and for another month the town would doze along peacefully.

Durham slumped himself into a chair that screeched protestingly in all its infirm joints. The heart was gone clean out of him.

"I don't understand these people at all," he confessed. "We're beating against a stone wall with our bare hands."

"If it should be money now that you're needing, Mr. Durham," spoke up Felsburg, "that boy Tandy's father was my very good friend when I first walked into that town with a peddling pack on my back, and if it should be money——?"

"It isn't money, Mr. Felsburg," said Durham. "If I didn't get a cent for my services I'd still fight this case out to the end for the sake of that game boy and that poor little mite of a wife of his. It isn't money or the lack of it—it's the damned hate they've built up here against the man. Why, you could cut it off in chunks—the prejudice that there was in that courthouse today."

"Son," put in Judge Priest in his high, weedy voice, "I reckon maybe you're right. I've been projectin' around cotehouses a good many years, and I've taken notice that when a jury look at a prisoner all the time and never look at his women folks it's a monstrous bad sign. And that's the way it was all day today."

"The judge will be fair—he always is," said Hightower, the local lawyer, "and of course Gilliam is only doing his duty. Those jurors are as good solid men as you can find in this country anywhere. But they can't help being prejudiced. Human nature's not strong enough to stand out against the feeling that's grown up round here against Tandy since he shot Ab Rankin."

"Son," said Judge Priest, still with his eyes on the darkening square below, "about how many of them jurors would you say are old soldiers?"

"Four or five that I know of," said Hightower—"and maybe more. It's hard to find a man over fifty years old in this section that didn't see active service in the Big War."

"Ah, hah," assented Judge Priest with a squeaky little grunt. "That foreman now—he looked like he might of seen some fightin'?"

"Four years of it," said Hightower. "He came out a captain in the cavalry."

"Ah, hah." Judge Priest sucked at his pipe.

"Herman," he wheezed back over his shoulder to Felsburg "did you notice a tall sort of a saddle-colored darky playing a juice harp in front of that there side-show as we came along up? I reckon that nigger could play almost any tune you'd a mind to hear him play?"

At a time like this Durham was distinctly not interested in the versatilities of strange negroes in this corner of the world. He kept silent, shrugging his shoulders petulantly.

"I wonder now is that nigger left town yet?" mused the old judge half to himself.

"I saw him just a while ago going down toward the depot," volunteered Hightower. "There's a train out of here for Memphis at 8:50. It's about twenty minutes of that now."

"Ah, hah, jest about," assented the judge. When the judge said "Ah, hah!" like that it sounded like the striking of a fiddle-bow across a fiddle's tautened E-string.

"Well, boys," he went on, "we've all got to do the best we can for Breck Tandy, ain't we? Say, son"—this was aimed at Durham—"I'd like mightily for you to put me on the stand the last one tomorrow. You wait until you're through with Herman and Colonel Quigley here, before you call me. And if I should seem to ramble somewhat in giving my testimony—why, son, you just let me ramble, will you? I know these people down here better maybe than you do—and if I should seem inclined to ramble, just let me go ahead and don't stop me, please?"

"Judge Priest," said Durham tartly, "if you think it could possibly do any good, ramble all you like."

"Much obliged," said the old judge, and he struggled into his low-quartered shoes and stood up, dusting the tobacco fluff off himself.

"Herman, have you got any loose change about you?"

Felsburg nodded and reached into his pocket. The judge made a discriminating selection of silver and bills from the handful that the merchant extended to him across the table.

"I'll take about ten dollars," he said. "I didn't come down here with more than enough to jest about buy my railroad ticket and pay my bill at this here tavern, and I might want a sweetenin' dram or somethin'."

He pouched his loan and crossed the room.

"Boys," he said, "I think I'll be knockin' round a little before I turn in. Herman, I may stop by your room a minute as I come back in. You boys better turn in early and git yourselves a good night's sleep. We are all liable to be purty tolerable busy tomorrow."

After he was outside he put his head back in the door and said to Durham:

"Remember, son, I may ramble."

Durham nodded shortly, being somewhat put out by the vagaries of a mind that could concern itself with trivial things on the imminent eve of a crisis.

As the judge creaked ponderously along the hall and down the stairs those he had left behind heard him whistling a tune to himself, making false starts at the air and halting often to correct his meter. It was an unknown tune to them all, but to Felsburg, the oldest of the four, it brought a vague, unplaced memory.

The old judge was whistling when he reached the street. He stood there a minute until he had mastered the tune to his own satisfaction, and then, still whistling, he shuffled along the uneven board pavement, which, after rippling up and down like a broken-backed snake, dipped downward to a little railroad station at the foot of the street.

.   .   .   .

In the morning nearly half the town—the white half—came to the trial, and enough of the black half to put a dark hem, like a mourning border, across the back width of the courtroom. Except that Main Street now drowsed in the heat where yesterday it had buzzed, this day might have been the day before. Again the resolute woodpecker drove his bloodied head with unimpaired energy against the tin sheathing up above. It was his third summer for that same cupola and the tin was pocked with little dents for three feet up and down. The mourning doves still pitched their lamenting note back and forth across the courthouse yard; and in the dewberry patch at the bottom of Aunt Tilly Haslett's garden down by the creek the meadow larks strutted in buff and yellow, with crescent-shaped gorgets of black at their throats, like Old Continentals, sending their clear-piped warning of "Laziness g'wine kill you!" in at the open windows of the steamy, smelly courtroom.

The defense lost no time getting under headway. As his main witness Durham called the prisoner to testify in his own behalf. Tandy gave his version of the killing with a frankness and directness that would have carried conviction to auditors more even-minded in their sympathies. He had gone to Rankin's office in the hope of bringing on a peaceful settlement of their quarrel. Rankin had flared up; had cursed him and advanced on him, making threats. Both of them reached for their guns then. Rankin's was the first out, but he fired first—that was all there was to it. Gilliam shone at cross-examination; he went at Tandy

savagely, taking hold like a snapping turtle and hanging on like one.

He made Tandy admit over and over again that
he carried a pistol habitually. In a community
where a third of the male adult population went armed
this admission was nevertheless taken as plain evidence of a nature bloody-minded and desperate. It
would have been just as bad for Tandy if he said he
armed himself especially for his visit to Rankin—
to these listeners that could have meant nothing else
but a deliberate, murderous intention. Either way
Gilliam had him, and he sweated in his eagerness to
bring out the significance of the point. A sinister
little murmuring sound, vibrant with menace, went
purring from bench to bench when Tandy told about
his pistol-carrying habit.

The cross-examination dragged along for hours. The
recess for dinner interrupted it; then it went on again,
Gilliam worrying at Tandy, goading at him, catching
him up and twisting his words. Tandy would not be
shaken, but twice under the manhandling he lost his
temper and lashed back at Gilliam, which was precisely what Gilliam most desired. A flary, fiery man,
prone to violent outbursts—that was the inference he
could draw from these blaze-ups.

It was getting on toward five o'clock before Gilliam
finally let his bedeviled enemy quit the witness-stand
and go back to his place between his wife and his
lawyer. As for Durham, he had little more to offer.
He called on Mr. Felsburg, and Mr. Felsburg gave
Tandy a good name as man and boy in his home town.
He called on Banker Quigley, who did the same thing
in different words. For these character witnesses
State's Attorney Gilliam had few questions. The case

was as good as won now, he figured; he could taste
already his victory over the famous lawyer from up
North, and he was greedy to hurry it forward.

The hot round hub of a sun had wheeled low enough
to dart its thin red spokes in through the westerly windows when Durham called his last witness. As Judge
Priest settled himself solidly in the witness chair with
the deliberation of age and the heft of flesh, the leveled
rays caught him full and lit up his round pink face,
with the short white-bleached beard below it and the
bald white-bleached forehead above. Durham eyed
him half doubtfully. He looked the image of a scatter-
witted old man, who would potter and philander round
a long time before he ever came to the point of anything. So he appeared to the others there, too. But
what Durham did not sense was that the homely simplicity of the old man was of a piece with the picture
of the courtroom, that he would seem to these watching, hostile people one of their own kind, and that they
would give to him in all likelihood a sympathy and understanding that had been denied the clothing merchant
and the broadclothed banker.

He wore a black alpaca coat that slanted upon him
in deep, longitudinal folds, and the front skirts of it
were twisted and pulled downward until they dangled
in long, wrinkly black teats. His shapeless gray
trousers were short for him and fitted his pudgy legs
closely. Below them dangled a pair of stout ankles
encased in white cotton socks and ending in low-
quarter black shoes. His shirt was clean but wrinkled
countlessly over his front. The gnawed and blackened
end of a cane pipestem stood out of his breast pocket,
rising like a frosted weed stalk.

He settled himself back in the capacious oak chair,

balanced upon his knees a white straw hat with a string
band round the crown and waited for the question.

"What is your name?" asked Durham.

"William Pitman Priest."

Even the voice somehow seemed to fit the setting.
Its high nasal note had a sort of whimsical appeal to it.

"When and where were you born?"

"In Calloway County, Kintucky, July 27, 1839."

"What is your profession or business?"

"I am an attorney-at-law."

"What position if any do you hold in your native
state?"

"I am presidin' judge of the first judicial district of
the state of Kintucky."

"And have you been so long?"

"For the past sixteen years."

"When were you admitted to the bar?"

"In 1860."

"And you have ever since been engaged, I take it,
either in the practise of the law before the bar or in its
administration from the bench?"

"Exceptin' for the four years from April, 1861, to
June, 1865."

Up until now Durham had been sparring, trying to
fathom the probable trend of the old judge's expected
meanderings. But in the answer to the last question
he thought he caught the cue and, tho none save
those two knew it, thereafter it was the witness who
led and the questioner who followed his lead blindly.

"And where were you during those four years?"

"I was engaged, suh, in takin' part in the war."

"The War of the Rebellion?"

"No, suh," the old man corrected him gently but
with firmness, "the War for the Southern Confederacy."

There was a least bit of a stir at this. Aunt Tilly's tape-edged palmleaf blade hovered a brief second in the wide regular arc of its sweep and the foreman of the jury involuntarily ducked his head, as if in affiance of an indubitable fact.

"Ahem!" said Durham, still feeling his way, altho now he saw the path more clearly. "And on which side were you engaged?"

"I was a private soldier in the Southern army," the old judge answered him, and as he spoke he straightened up.

"Yes, suh," he repeated, "for four years I was a private soldier in the late Southern Confederacy. Part of the time I was down here in this very country," he went on as tho he had just recalled that part of it. "Why, in the summer of '64 I was right here in this town. And until yistiddy I hadn't been back since."

He turned to the trial judge and spoke to him with a tone and manner half apologetic, half confidential.

"Your Honor," he said, "I am a judge myself, occupyin' in my home state a position very similar to the one which you fill here, and whilst I realize, none better, that this ain't all accordin' to the rules of evidence as laid down in the books, yet when I git to thinkin' about them old soldierin' times I find I am inclined to sort of reminiscence round a little. And I trust your Honor will pardon me if I should seem to ramble slightly?"

His tone was more than apologetic and more than confidential. It was winning. The judge upon the bench was a veteran himself. He looked toward the prosecutor.

"Has the state's attorney any objection to this line of testimony?" he asked, smiling a little.

Certainly Gilliam had no fear that this honest-appearing old man's wanderings could damage a case already as good as won. He smiled back indulgently and waved his arm with a gesture that was compounded of equal parts of toleration and patience, with a top-dressing of contempt. "I fail," said Gilliam, "to see wherein the military history and achievements of this worthy gentleman can possibly affect the issue of the homicide of Abner J. Rankin. But," he added magnanimously, "if the defense chooses to encumber the record with matters so trifling and irrelevant I surely will make no objection now or hereafter."

"The witness may proceed," said the judge.

"Well, really, Your Honor, I didn't have so very much to say," confessed Judge Priest, "and I didn't expect there'd be any to-do made over it. What I was trying to git at was that comin' down here to testify in this case sort of brought back them old days to my mind. As I git along more in years—" he was looking toward the jurors now—"I find that I live more and more in the past."

As tho he had put a question to them several of the jurors gravely inclined their heads. The busy cud of Juror No. 12 moved just a trifle slower in its travels from the right side of the jaw to the left and back again.

"Yes, suh," he said musingly, "I got up early this mornin' at the tavern where I'm stoppin' and took a walk through your thrivin' little city." This was rambling with a vengeance, thought the puzzled Durham. "I walked down here to a bridge over a little creek and back again. It reminded me mightily of that other time when I passed through this town—in '64— just about this season of the year—and it was hot early today just as it was that other time—and the dew was thick on the grass, the same as 'twas then."

He halted a moment.

"Of course your town didn't look the same this mornin' as it did that other mornin'. It seemed like to me there are twicet as many houses here now as there used to be—it's got to be quite a little city."

Mr. Lukins, the grocer, nodded silent approval of this utterance, Mr. Lukins having but newly completed and moved into a two-story brick store building with a tin cornice and an outside staircase.

"Yes, suh, your town has grown mightily, but"— and the whiny, humorous voice grew apologetic again— "but your roads are purty much the same as they were in '64—hilly in places—and kind of rocky."

Durham found himself sitting still, listening hard. Everybody else was listening too. Suddenly it struck Durham, almost like a blow, that this simple old man had somehow laid a sort of spell upon them all. The flattening sunrays made a kind of pink glow about the old judge's face, touching gently his bald head and his white whiskers. He droned on:

"I remember about those roads particularly well, because that time when I marched through here in '64 my feet was about out of my shoes and them flints cut 'em up some. Some of the boys, I recollect, left bloody prints in the dust behind 'em. But shucks—it wouldn't a-made no real difference if we'd a-wore the bottoms plum off our feet! We'd a-kept on goin'. We'd a-gone anywhere—or tried to—behind old Bedford Forrest."

Aunt Tilly's palmleaf halted in air and the twelfth juror's faithful quid froze in his cheek and stuck there like a small wen. Except for a general hunching for-

ward of shoulders and heads there was no movement
anywhere and no sound except the voice of the witness:

"Old Bedford Forrest hisself was leadin' us, and
so naturally we just went along with him, shoes or no
shoes. There was a regiment of Northern troops—
Yankees—marchin' on this town that mornin', and it
seemed the word had traveled ahead of 'em that they
was aimin' to burn it down.

"Probably it wasn't true. When we got to know
them Yankees better afterward we found out that there
really wasn't no difference, to speak of, between
the run of us and the run of them. Probably it wasn't
so at all. But in them days the people were prone
to believe 'most anything—about Yankees—and the
word was that they was comin' across country, a-burn-
in' and cuttin' and slashin', and the people here
thought they was going to be burned out of house and
home. So old Bedford Forrest he marched all night
with a battalion of us—four companies—Kintuckians
and Tennesseeans mostly, with a sprinklin' of boys
from Mississippi and Arkansas—some of us ridin' and
some walkin' afoot, like me—we didn't always have
horses enough to go round that last year. And somehow we got here before they did. It was a close race
tho between us—them a-comin' down from the
North and us a-comin' up from the other way. We
met 'em down there by that little branch just below
where your present railroad depot is. There wasn't no
depot there then, but the branch looks just the same
now as it did then—and the bridge too. I walked
acros't it this mornin' to see. Yes, suh, right there
was where we met 'em. And there was a right smart
fight.

"Yes, suh, there was a right smart fight for about

twenty minutes—or maybe twenty-five—and then we had breakfast."

He had been smiling gently as he went along. Now he broke into a throaty little chuckle.

"Yes, suh, it all come back to me this mornin'—every little bit of it—the breakfast and all. I didn't have much breakfast, tho, as I recall—none of us did—probably just corn pone and branch water to wash it down with." And he wiped his mouth with the back of his hand as tho the taste of the gritty corn-meal cakes was still there.

There was another little pause here; the witness seemed to be through. Durham's crisp question cut the silence like a gash with a knife.

"Judge Priest, do you know the defendant at the bar, and if so, how well do you know him?"

"I was just comin' to that," he answered with simplicity, "and I'm obliged to you for puttin' me back on the track. Oh, I know the defendant at the bar mighty well—as well as anybody on earth ever did know him, I reckon, unless 'twas his own maw and paw. I've known him, in fact, from the time he was born—and a gentler, better-disposed boy never grew up in our town. His nature seemed almost too sweet for a boy—more like a girl's—but as a grown man he was always manly, and honest, and fair—and not quarrelsome. Oh, yes, I know him. I knew his father and his mother before him. It's a funny thing too—comin' up this way—but I remember that his paw was marchin' right alongside of me the day we came through here in '64. He was wounded, his paw was, right at the edge of that little creek down yonder. He was wounded in the shoulder—and he never did entirely git over it."

Again he stopped dead short, and he lifted his hand and tugged at the lobe of his right ear absently. Simultaneously Mr. Felsburg, who was sitting close to a window beyond the jury box, was also seized with nervousness, for he jerked out a handkerchief and with it mopped his brow so vigorously that, to one standing outside, it might have seemed that the handkerchief was actually being waved about as a signal.

Instantly then there broke upon the pause that still endured a sudden burst of music, a rollicking, jingling air. It was only a twenty-cent mouth organ, three sleigh bells, and a pair of rib bones of a beef-cow being played all at once by a saddle-colored negro man but it sounded for all the world like a fife-and-drum corps:

> *If you want to have a good time,*
> *If you want to have a good time,*
> *If you want to have a good time,*
> *If you want to ketch the devil—*
> *Jine the cavalree!*

To some who heard it now the tune was strange; these were the younger ones. But to those older men and the older women the first jubilant bars rolled back the years like a scroll.

> *If you want to have a good time,*
> *If you want to have a good time,*
> *If you want to have a good time,*
> *If you want to ride with Bedford—*
> *Jine the cavalree!*

The sound swelled and rippled and rose through the windows—the marching song of the Southern trooper—

Forrest's men, and Morgan's, and Jeb Stuart's and Joe Wheeler's. It had in it the jingle of saber chains, the creak of sweaty saddle-girths, the nimble clunk of hurrying hoofs. It had in it the clanging memories of a cause and a time that would live with these people as long as they lived and their children lived and their children's children. It had in it the one sure call to the emotions and the sentiments of these people.

And it rose and rose and then as the unseen minstrel went slouching down Main Street, toward the depot and the creek, it sank lower and became a thin thread of sound, and then a broken thread of sound, and then it died out altogether and once more there was silence in the courthouse of Forked Deer County.

Strangely enough not one listener had come to the windows to look out. The interruption from without had seemed part and parcel of what went on within. None faced to the rear, every one faced to the front.

There was Mr. Lukins now. As Mr. Lukins got upon his feet he said to himself in a tone of feeling that he be dad-fetched. But immediately changing his mind he stated that he would preferably be dad-blamed, and as he moved toward the bar rail one over-hearing him might have gathered from remarks let fall that Mr. Lukins was going somewhere with the intention of being extensively dad-burned. But for all these threats Mr. Lukins didn't go anywhere, except as near the railing as he could press.

Nearly everybody else was standing up too. The state's attorney was on his feet with the rest, seemingly for the purpose of making some protest.

Had any one looked they might have seen that the ember in the smoldering eye of the old foreman had blazed up to a brown fire; that Juror No. 4, with utter disregard for expense, was biting segments out of the brim of his new brown-varnished straw hat; that No. 7 had dropped his crutches on the floor, and that no one, not even their owner, had heard them fall; that all the jurors were half out of their chairs. But no one saw these things, for at this moment there rose up Aunt Tilly Haslett, a dominant figure, her huge wide back blocking the view of three or four immediately behind her.

Uncle Fayette laid a timid detaining hand upon her and seemed to be saying something protestingly.

"Turn lose of me, Fate Haslett!" she commanded. "Ain't you ashamed of yourse'f, to be tryin' to hold me back when you know how my only dear brother died a-followin' after Gineral Nathan Bedford Forrest. Turn loose of me!"

She flirted her great arm and Uncle Fayette spun flutteringly into the mass behind. The sheriff barred her way at the gate of the bar.

"Mizz Haslett," he implored, "please, Mizz Haslett— you must keep order in the cote."

Aunt Tilly halted in her onward move, head up high and elbows out, and through her specs, blazing like burning-glasses, she fixed on him a look that instantly charred that unhappy official into a burning red ruin of his own self-importance.

"Keep it yourse'f, High Sheriff Washington Nash, Esquire," she bade him; "that's whut you git paid good money for doin'. And git out of my way! I'm a-goin' in there to that pore little lonesome thing settin' there all by herself, and there ain't nobody goin' to hinder me neither!"

The sheriff shrunk aside; perhaps it would be better to say he evaporated aside. And public opinion, re-

organized and made over but still incarnate in Aunt
Tilly Haslett, swept past the rail and settled like a
billowing black cloud into a chair that the local attorney for the defense vacated just in time to save himself the inconvenience of having it snatched bodily
from under him.

"There, honey," said Aunt Tilly crooningly as she
gathered the forlorn little figure of the prisoner's wife
in her arms like a child and mothered her up to her
ample bombazined bosom, "there now, honey, you jest
cry on me."

Then Aunt Tilly looked up and her specs were all
blurry and wet. But she waved her palmleaf fan as
tho it had been the baton of a marshal.

"Now, Jedge," she said, addressing the bench, "and
you other gentlemen—you kin go ahead now."

The state's attorney had meant evidently to make
some sort of an objection, for he was upon his feet
through all this scene. But he looked back before
he spoke and what he saw kept him from speaking.
I believe I stated earlier that he was a candidate for
reelection. So he settled back down in his chair and
stretched out his legs and buried his chin in the top
of his limp white waistcoat in an attitude that he had
once seen in a picture entitled, "Napoleon Bonaparte
at St. Helena."

"You may resume, Judge Priest," said the trial
judge in a voice that was not entirely free from huski-
ness, altho its owner had been clearing it steadily for
some moments.

"Thank you kindly, suh, but I was about through
anyhow," answered the witness with a bow, and for
all his homeliness there was dignity and stateliness in
it. "I merely wanted to say for the sake of completin'

the record, so to speak, that on the occasion referred to
them Yankees did not cross that bridge."

With the air of tendering and receiving congratu-
lations Mr. Lukins turned to his nearest neighbor and
shook hands with him warmly.

The witness got up somewhat stiffly, once more
becoming a commonplace old man in a wrinkled black
alpaca coat, and made his way back to his vacant place,
now in the shadow of Aunt Tilly Haslett's form. As
he passed along the front of the jury-box the foreman's
crippled right hand came up in a sort of a clumsy
salute, and the juror at the other end of the rear
row—No. 12, the oldest juror—leaned forward as if
to speak to him, but remembered in time where his
present duty lay. The old judge kept on until he came
to Durham's side and he whispered to him:

"Son, they've quit lookin' at him and they're all
a-lookin' at her. Son, rest your case."

Durham came out of a maze.

"Your Honor," he said as he arose, "the defense
rests."

.   .   .   .

The jury were out only six minutes. Mr. Lukins
insisted that it was only five minutes and a half, and
added that he'd be dad-rotted if it was a second longer
than that.

As the lately accused Tandy came out of the courthouse with his imported lawyer—Aunt Tilly bringing up the rear with his trembling, weeping, happy
little wife—friendly hands were outstretched to clasp
his and a whiskered old gentleman with a thumbnail
like a Brazil nut grabbed at his arm.

"Whichaway did Billy Priest go?" he demanded—

"little old Fightin' Billy—whar did he go to? Soon as he started in talkin' I placed him. Whar is he?"

Walking side by side, Tandy and Durham came down the steps into the soft June night, and Tandy took a long, deep breath into his lungs.

"Mr. Durham," he said, "I owe a great deal to you."

"How's that?" said Durham.

Just ahead of them, centered in a shaft of light from the window of the barroom of the Drummers' Home Hotel, stood Judge Priest. The old judge had been drinking. The pink of his face was a trifle more pronounced, the high whine in his voice a trifle weedier, as he counted one by one certain pieces of silver into a wide-open palm of a saddle-colored negro.

"How's that?" said Durham.

"I say I owe everything in the world to you," repeated Tandy.

"No," said Durham, "what you owe me is the fee you agreed to pay me for defending you. There's the man you're looking for."

And he pointed to the old judge.

HIS FIRST PENITENT

By James Oliver Curwood

Chapter I

In a white wilderness of moaning storm, in a wilderness of miles and miles of black pine-trees, the Transcontinental Flier lay buried in the snow.

In the first darkness of the wild December night, engine and tender had rushed on ahead to division headquarters, to let the line know that the flier had given up the fight. and needed assistance. They had been gone two hours, and whiter and whiter grew the brilliantly lighted coaches in the drifts and winnows of the whistling storm. From the black edges of the forest, prowling eyes might have looked upon scores of human faces staring anxiously out into the blackness from the windows of the coaches.

In those coaches it was growing steadily colder. Men were putting on their overcoats, and women snuggled deeper in their furs. Over it all, the tops of the black pine-trees moaned and whistled in sounds that seemed filled both with menace and with savage laughter.

In the smoking-compartment of the Pullman sat five men, gathered in a group. Of these, one was Forsythe, the timber agent; two were traveling men; the fourth a passenger homeward bound from a holiday visit; and the fifth was Father Charles.

All were smoking, and had been smoking for an hour, even to Father Charles, who lighted his third cigar as one of the traveling men finished the story he had been telling. They had passed away the tedious wait with tales of personal adventure and curious happenings. Each had furnished his share of entertainment, with the exception of Father Charles.

The priest's pale, serious face lit up in surprize or laughter with the others, but his lips had not broken into a story of their own. He was a little man, dressed in somber black, and there was that about him which told his companions that within his tight-drawn coat of shiny black there were hidden tales which would have gone well with the savage beat of the storm against lighted windows and the moaning tumult of the pine-trees.

Suddenly Forsythe shivered at a fiercer blast than the others, and said:

"Father, have you a text that would fit this night—and the situation?"

Slowly Father Charles blew out a spiral of smoke from between his lips, and then he drew himself erect and leaned a little forward, with the cigar between his slender white fingers.

"I had a text for this night," he said, "but I have none now, gentlemen. I was to have married a couple a hundred miles down the line. The guests have assembled. They are ready, but I am not there. The wedding will not be to-night, and so my text is gone. But there comes another to my mind which fits this situation—and a thousand others—'He who sits in the heavens shall look down and decide.' To-night I was to have married these young people. Three hours ago I never dreamed of doubting that I should be on

hand at the appointed hour. But I shall not marry
them. Fate has enjoined a hand. The Supreme Arbiter says 'No,' and what may not be the consequences?"

"They will probably be married to-morrow," said
one of the traveling men. "There will be a few hours'
delay—nothing more."

"Perhaps," replied Father Charles, as quietly as before. "And—perhaps not. Who can say what this
little incident may not mean in the lives of that young
man and that young woman—and, it may be, in my
own? Three or four hours lost in a storm—what may
they not mean to more than one human heart on this
train? The Supreme Arbiter plays His hand, if you
wish to call it that, with reason and intent. To some
one, somewhere, the most insignificant occurrence may
mean life or death. And to-night—this—means something."

A sudden blast drove the night screeching over their
heads, and the wailing of the pines was almost human
voices. Forsythe sucked a cigar that had gone out.

"Long ago," said Father Charles, "I knew a young
man and a young woman who were to be married. The
man went West to win a fortune. Thus fate separated them, and in the lapse of a year such terrible
misfortune came to the girl's parents that she was
forced into a marriage with wealth—a barter of her
white body for an old man's gold. When the young
man returned from the West he found his sweetheart
married, and hell upon earth was their lot. But hope
lingers in young hearts. He waited four years; and
then, discouraged, he married another woman. Gentlemen, *three days* after the wedding his old sweetheart's
husband died, and she was released from bondage.

Was not that the hand of the Supreme Arbiter? If he had waited but three days more, the old happiness might have lived.

"But wait! One month after that day the young man was arrested, taken to a Western State, tried for murder, and hanged. Do you see the point? In three days more the girl who had sold herself into slavery for the salvation of those she loved would have been released from her bondage only to marry a murderer!"

Chapter II

There was a silence, in which all five listened to that wild moaning of the storm. There seemed to be something in it now—something more than the inarticulate sound of wind and trees. Forsythe scratched a match and relighted his cigar.

"I never thought of such things in just that light," he said.

"Listen to the wind," said the little priest. "Hear the pine-trees shriek out there! It recalls to me a night of years and years ago—a night like this, when the storm moaned and twisted about my little cabin, and when the Supreme Arbiter sent me my first penitent. Gentlemen, it is something which will bring you nearer to an understanding of the voice and the hand of God. It is a sermon on the mighty significance of little things, this story of my first penitent. If you wish, I will tell it to you."

"Go on," said Forsythe.

The traveling men drew nearer.

"It was a night like this," repeated Father Charles, "and it was in a great wilderness like this, only miles and miles away. I had been sent to establish a mission; and in my cabin, that wild night, alone and with the storm shrieking about me, I was busy at work sketching out my plans. After a time I grew nervous. I did not smoke then, and so I had nothing to comfort me but my thoughts; and, in spite of my efforts to make them otherwise, they were cheerless enough. The forest grew to my door. In the fiercer blasts I could hear the lashing of the pine-tops over my head, and now and then an arm of one of the moaning trees would reach down and sweep across my cabin roof with a sound that made me shudder and fear. This wilderness fear is an oppressive and terrible thing when you are alone at night, and the world is twisting and tearing itself outside. I have heard the pine-trees shriek like dying women, I have heard them wailing like lost children, I have heard them sobbing and moaning like human souls writhing in agony—"

Father Charles paused, to peer through the window out into the black night, where the pine-trees were sobbing and moaning now. When he turned, Forsythe, the timber agent, whose life was a wilderness life, nodded understandingly.

"And when they cry like that," went on Father Charles, "a living voice would be lost among them as the splash of a pebble is lost in a roaring sea. A hundred times that night I fancied that I heard human voices; and a dozen times I went to my door, drew back the bolt, and listened, with the snow and the wind beating about my ears.

"As I sat shuddering before my fire, there came a thought to me of a story which I had long ago read about the sea—a story of impossible achievement and of impossible heroism. As vividly as if I had read it only the day before, I recalled the description of a wild and stormy night when the heroine placed a lighted lamp in the window of her sea-bound cottage, to guide her lover home in safety. Gentlemen, the reading of that book in my boyhood days was but a trivial thing. I had read a thousand others, and of them all it was possibly the least significant; but the Supreme Arbiter had not forgotten.

"The memory of that book brought me to my feet, and I placed a lighted lamp close up against my cabin window. Fifteen minutes later I heard a strange sound at the door, and when I opened it there fell in upon the floor at my feet a young and beautiful woman. And after her, dragging himself over the threshold on his hands and knees, there came a man.

"I closed the door, after the man had crawled in and fallen face downward upon the floor, and turned my attention first to the woman. She was covered with snow. Her long, beautiful hair was loose and disheveled, and had blown about her like a veil. Her big, dark eyes looked at me pleadingly, and in them there was a terror such as I had never beheld in human eyes before. I bent over her, intending to carry her to my cot; but in another moment she had thrown herself upon the prostrate form of the man, with her arms about his head, and there burst from her lips the first sounds that she had uttered. They were not much more intelligible than the wailing grief of the pine-trees out in the night, but they told me plainly enough that the man on the floor was dearer to her than life.

"I knelt beside him, and found that he was breathing in a quick, panting sort of way, and that his wide-open eyes were looking at the woman. Then I noticed for the first time that his face was cut and bruised, and his lips were swollen. His coat was loose at the throat, and I could see livid marks on his neck.

" 'I'm all right,' he whispered, struggling for breath, and turning his eyes to me. 'We should have died—in a few minutes more—if it hadn't been for the light in your window!'

"The young woman bent down and kissed him, and then she allowed me to help her to my cot. When I had attended to the young man, and he had regained strength enough to stand upon his feet, she was asleep. The man went to her, and dropped upon his knees beside the cot. Tenderly he drew back the heavy masses of hair from about her face and shoulders. For several minutes he remained with his face pressed close against hers; then he rose, and faced me. The woman—his wife—knew nothing of what passed between us during the next half-hour. During that half-hour, gentlemen, I received my first confession. The young man was of my faith. He was my first penitent."

It was growing colder in the coach, and Father Charles stopped to draw his thin black coat closer about him. Forsythe relighted his cigar for the third time. The transient passenger gave a sudden start as a gust of wind beat against the window like a threatening hand.

"A rough stool was my confessional, gentlemen," resumed Father Charles. "He told me the story, kneeling at my feet—a story that will live with me as long as I live, always reminding me that the little things of life may be the greatest things, that by sending a storm to hold up a coach the Supreme Arbiter may change the map of a world. It is not a long story. It is not even an unusual story.

"He had come into the North about a year before, and had built for himself and his wife a little home at a pleasant river spot ten miles from my cabin. Their love was of the kind we do not often see, and they were as happy as the birds that lived about them in the wilderness. They had taken a timber claim. A few months more, and a new life was to come into their little home; and the knowledge of this made the girl an angel of beauty and joy. Their nearest neighbor was another man, several miles distant. The two men became friends, and the other came over to see them frequently. It was the old, old story. The neighbor fell in love with the young settler's wife.

"As you shall see, this other man was a beast. On the day preceding that night of terrible storm, the woman's husband set out for the settlement to bring back supplies. Hardly had he gone, when the beast came to the cabin. He found himself alone with the woman.

"A mile from his cabin, the husband stopped to light his pipe. See, gentlemen, how the Supreme Arbiter played His hand. The man attempted to unscrew the stem, and the stem broke. In the wilderness you must smoke. Smoke is your company. It is voice and companionship to you. There were other pipes at the settlement, ten miles away; but there was also another pipe at the cabin, one mile away. So the husband turned back. He came up quietly to his door, thinking that he would surprize his wife. He heard voices— a man's voice, a woman's cries. He opened the door, and in the excitement of what was happening within neither the man nor the woman saw or heard him.

They were struggling. The woman was in the man's arms, her hair torn down, her small hands beating him in the face, her breath coming in low, terrified cries. Even as the husband stood there for the fraction of a second, taking in the terrible scene, the other man caught the woman's face to him, and kissed her. And then—it happened. It was a terrible fight; and when it was over the beast lay on the floor, bleeding and dead. Gentlemen, the Supreme Arbiter *broke a pipe-stem*, and sent the husband back in time!"

Chapter III

No one spoke as Father Charles drew his coat still closer about him. Above the tumult of the storm another sound came to them—the distant, piercing shriek of a whistle.

"The husband dug a grave through the snow and in the frozen earth," concluded Father Charles; "and late that afternoon they packed up a bundle and set out together for the settlement. The storm overtook them. They had dropped for the last time into the snow, about to die in each other's arms, when I put my light in the window. That is all; except that I knew them for several years afterward, and that the old happiness returned to them—and more, for the child was born, a miniature of its mother. Then they moved to another part of the wilderness, and I to still another. So you see, gentlemen, what a snow-bound train may mean, for if an old sea tale, a broken pipe-stem—"

The door at the end of the smoking-room opened suddenly. Through it there came a cold blast of the storm, a cloud of snow, and a man. He was bundled

in a great bearskin coat, and as he shook out its folds
his strong, ruddy face smiled cheerfully at those whom
he had interrupted.

Then, suddenly, there came a change in his face.
The merriment went from it. He stared at Father
Charles.

The priest was rising, his face more tense and
whiter still, his hands reaching out to the stranger.

In another moment the stranger had leaped to him—
not to shake his hands, but to clasp the priest in his
great arms, shaking him, and crying out a strange
joy, while for the first time that night the pale face
of Father Charles was lighted up with a red and joyous
glow.

After several minutes the newcomer released Father
Charles, and turned to the others with a great, hearty
laugh.

"Gentlemen," he said, "you must pardon me for
interrupting you like this. You will understand when
I tell you that Father Charles is an old friend of mine,
the dearest friend I have on earth, and that I haven't
seen him for years. I was his first penitent!"

STRAIN

By ALBERT RICHARD WETJEN

A strong wind blew over the sand-dunes from seaward and crisped the dull water of the bay. Right
across the gap through the dunes, where the sea entered, the breakers roared white and high. When each
broke, a chaos of foam spread into the bay and drifted
well-nigh to the wharves of the little port on the farther
shore. The sky was dull and cloudy. The sun came
out at rare intervals and then disappeared. Occa-
sionally a slight drizzle whisked down wind and then
ceased. Beyond the white breakers came the muffled
cry of a whistling buoy.

Dotted here and there over the bay, like great un-
shapely cakes, sand-banks lifted their smooth sides from
the swirl of the outgoing tide. A tiny ferry wended a
snorting way across the water. A small barkentine
was anchored between two wet sand-banks, a lean rusty-
gray barkentine. Her canvas hung in bights from her
foremast yards. Her main and mizzen canvas was
heaped up on the midship and after-deck. Her fore-
deck was a clutter of cargo. Desolate she looked in
the rain.

Alongside the rickety pile-built wharves of the town
lay three ships. Two were steam schooners, built of
steel, loading lumber for coastal ports. The officers of
these small vessels were busy at work with the seamen

loading slings, driving winches, unrecognizable to a
stranger as officers.

The third ship was of wood. Her squat hull had
been painted so often, layer over layer, that the plank
edges could hardly be seen. Her two masts were
stumpy and thick. It was apparent, from the two metal
hoops that remained at their trucks, that they had been
built to carry topmasts, built for the strain of canvas
and criss-crossed rigging. Now they were bare, save
for derrick falls. Instead of canvas, steam turned a
screw and drove her. She was a converted "wind-
jammer."

Her bridge was midships, unlike those on the
schooners whose bridges were aft, a long flat bridge.
The fore-deck was enormously deep below the iron
bulwarks. Cargo cluttered it. Many hatches broke it
up. The fo'c's'le-head, whereunder the small crew
existed, was very tiny, as tho the builders begrudged
the space for the seaman to live in. New paint, shining
and bright, covered the ship's age. It saved her from
the desolate appearance of the anchored barkentine.

A few coastal passengers, men and women, lounged
over the for'ard bridge-rail and watched the men busy
in the holds below. The winches rattled monotonously,
mingling with the winches from the steam schooners
and the noise of the elements. The cargo waiting on
the ancient wharf was lifted, sling-load by sling-load,
into the ship's gaping stomach. Men swore as they
worked.

The predominating thing was noise. Men shouted.
The ship's officers—they could be distinguished by their
uniform suits and gold braid—did not work with the
seamen. They superintended, as officers should. Because their ship had been remodelled from a pure

freighter to accommodate passengers, it was deemed that the officers must be in future always officers, in dress and deportment, a very faint echo of the super-smartness of the officers who cluttered the bridges of transatlantic packets.

Up the nearly level gangway the agent for the company who owned the ship pushed his way. He was a tall man, dressed in tweeds. He looked neat and prosperous. His face was thin; so were his lips. In his right hand he carried a packet of papers. With his left he thrust aside seamen and passengers as he made for the bridge. He found the captain in his room laboriously writing a letter. He entered without knocking, arrogantly. Bitter lines creased his face from nose to mouth corners.

"Captain," he said sharply, "you'll have to move to wharf three right away."

The captain laid down his pen deliberately and swung round in his swivel-chair.

"Good morning, Mr. Agent. Sit down," he said. He waved to the faded red settee that stood against the bulkhead near the door.

"Haven't time!" The agent's voice was irritable. "Right away, captain," he repeated.

The captain grunted. He was a stout man with a face like a full moon. His complexion was a deep red, a dusky red, a red that had taken the sun and wind many years to produce. The captain's eye was small and somewhat dull, yellowish as to white. His mouth was big-lipped, protruding. His shoulders were vast, seeming to tighten the threadbare serge jacket he wore. His hair was sparse and gray; his red neck showed, vividly clear and criss-crossed with clefts, against the fringe of bristles that ran beneath his coat-collar. His voice was deep and even, husky somewhat, but with a hint of unbelievable power. You could never imagine any noise occurring that would drown out his voice.

"Sit down," he repeated, then grumbled, "I never knew a time I come to this port but what I don't have to shift ship about every other day."

"That's not my fault," the agent shrilled. "I have to get you loaded with all speed. I have to cut cost. It's cheaper to move ship than to move cargo from one wharf to another."

"Eh, I suppose." The captain sighed and frowned. His face went a little redder. "For the sake of five dollars owners'll do anything. They seem to think a ship's like a motor-truck, to be taken anywhere at any time."

"Well, what about it?" the agent's reedy voice persisted. He snarled a little. "I can't help that. You've got to move. What you got to kick about, anyway? You ain't doing nothing."

The captain's face set. "Oh, no," he admitted. "I never do anything. Soft life I've got. Two hundred a month and no work. Easy life. . . . I wish some of you fellers'd take a ship over this bar, f'r instance. No work. Oh, no. Seems simple, don't it, t' stand on the bridge and give orders? Oh, yes."

"Well," shrilled the agent, "there's plenty of captains who'd be only too glad of your job. If you want to quit, just say so."

"That's so." The captain sighed. "But I've a wife and children. . . . When do I have to move?"

"Right away. The sooner the better. Don't think you can wait. I want the ship moved now."

"And I suppose after I've moved I'll have to move back, eh, same as usual?"

"I don't know. What if you do? Am I the agent or
are you? It's up to me to get the cargo aboard. I get
the blame if it isn't all aboard. What's it to you, heh,
so long as you get paid and fed?"

"All right. But I'm the one who gets blamed for
slow voyages and injuries to my ship. Have you
thought it's low tide now? How do I know there's
water enough for me to shift? You know these sand-
banks are always changing. Have you thought of this
blasted wind blowing from seaward, and the tide sweeping out? . . . You fellers always come at the worst
time to move a ship."

"You'll do as you're told, captain, or I'll report you
to the owners. I want the ship moved now. Why,
wharf three is only a hundred yards down. I'm not
asking you to cross the bay."

"Oh, no." The captain rose wearily from his chair
and put his uniform cap on his head. He sighed. It
was so useless to make a landsman see the difficulties.
And it was true there were so many master mariners
out of work. Any of them would be glad of a job.
Preceding the captain, the agent went out on deck
whining complaints and threats.

The captain ascended the tiny navigation-bridge and,
crossing to the brass speaking-tube to the engine-room,
whistled down. The engineer on watch answered.

"How soon can you give me steam?" asked the captain. The engineer grew profane. He wanted to know
what was the matter with several things.

"I've got to move ship," the captain explained
wearily. "The agent's here stewing about. . . ."

"That's right, blame it on me," whined the agent,

who had followed the captain on to the bridge. "I'll send in a report to the owners."

The captain growled, "Oh, shut up," as he jammed back the plug in the tube mouthpiece.

He leaned over the bridge-rail and bawled down to the fore-deck.

"Mr. Leach!"

The mate looked up. He was standing by the combing of number three hatch and intently watching to see that none of the stevedores below broached the incoming cargo. "Sir?" he shouted back.

The captain cupped his hands round his mouth, for the derricks were rattling fearsomely.

"Swing those booms inboard! We've got to move ship!"

The mate shouted, "Again! G' damn!" and then turned away and shouted to his seaman for'ard. The captain called a steward from the bridge-deck below.

"Get hold of the second mate," he said.

"He's ashore," said the steward.

"Where's the third mate?"

"He's ashore too, sir."

"Confound! Can't they stay aboard five minutes in port? That's the worst of young officers when you're carrying wimmin passengers. . . . All right, steward, that'll do. . . . See here, Mr. Agent, the sort of jam you run me into? I haven't an officer aboard saving the mate."

The agent sneered. He shrilled triumphantly, "Well, you ought to have. What do you let them go ashore for? The ship's got to be moved, and that's all there is to it."

The captain turned deliberately. His eyes blazed.

"See here, Mr. Agent. When my officers are at sea

they stand their watch, four-on and eight-off. And they do their duty. When they're in port they stand the same watches. Do you expect them to be with the damned ship night and day? Keep your mouth shut or I kick you ashore. My mates are off watch and they've every right to go ashore unless I tell 'em not to."

The agent exploded. He waved his fists aloft. "Keep my mouth shut? Confound you, captain. Don't you talk to me like that. I'll report . . ."

"Oh, shut up!" the captain said wearily, and turned away. His hands gripped the bridge-rail before him. Often he had a hard job at control. Many were the times he would be willing to give a month's pay to hit a ship's agent or owner for stupid pigheadedness. But he had a wife and a family. He turned after a while and faced the fuming agent.

"Would you mind going below while we shift ship?" he inquired with elaborate politeness. The agent muttered sullenly and, without answering, strode towards the bridge-companion and went down.

The captain grunted, muttered an oath, and then crossed to where the siren lanyard hung alongside the little closed-in chart-house. He jerked angrily on the cord and the siren boomed, drowning all other noise and echoing back and forth across the bay. If either the second or the third mate was in hearing, he would return to the ship at that signal.

The mate came on the bridge swearing profusely. He had left the bos'n on the fore-deck below to see to the derricks. The rattle of the winches was now less frequent as the great booms were swung inboard and their guys drawn taut.

"What's the big idea?" the mate inquired. The cap-

tain jammed his hands into his side pockets and shook
his head.

"Search me," he said. "But you know what it is in
this blamed port. We always move about twice a day.
Trouble is, the agent hasn't enough savvey to gather
all cargo on one wharf before we arrive. Pah! Makes
me sick."

"Where we going, sir?"

"Wharf three."

"Guess the second and third are ashore too, eh?"

"So the steward said."

"Why the devil couldn't that agent have let us know
last night or something?" the mate grumbled. He lit
a cigaret and sulked. The captain pulled out his pipe
and cleaned the bowl noisily with his knife. "Damn!"
he said, scowling, and then for a while both men were
silent.

One of the loading steam schooners lay ahead of the
ship, between her and wharf three. Had the schooner
not been there, it would have been merely a matter of
the ship being pulled along to the desired wharf by
means of hawsers attached to the shore bollards and
shifted as the ship hauled up on them. But with the
schooner in the way, the ship would have to cast free
from the wharf entirely and steam round the schooner.
Then she would have to haul in to number three wharf
and make fast.

At high tide and in normal weather, the maneuver
would not have presented much difficulty. But with
low tide and in a bay where the water depths varied
and no sand-bank was stationary, the task was one full
of anxiety. Also the wind blew ever stronger from
seaward. Also the outrunning tide created a rip that

sagged heavily at anything afloat that left the shelter of the wharf.

"Stand by," rang the captain on the brass telegraphs to the engine-room. The answering jangle came back. The captain leaned over the bridge and shouted down to the mate, who was on the fo'c'sle-head with the port watch.

"Man at the wheel!"

The mate lifted his hand to show he had heard.

"Man at the wheel," he said to the bos'n.

"Man at the wheel," repeated the bos'n to the three men of the watch. The men looked at each other.

"Your wheel, Shorty," said one, spitting tobacco-juice overside with a swift turn of his head.

"Guess that's so," mumbled Shorty, and he waddled down the ladder from the fo'c'sle-head to the fore-deck and so to the bridge. When he was finally ensconced on the grating in the wheel-house, the captain peered down at him through the open for'ard window of the chart-house and through the aperture in the house-floor.

"All ready?" said the captain.

"All ready, sir," Shorty assured him. The captain grunted.

"Then put your helm midships."

"Midship helm," repeated Shorty. He turned the wheel-spokes.

The captain went to the bridge-rail and peered aft.

"Let go, Mr. Murphy! Hold her with the spring!" he shouted to the third mate, who had come aboard in response to the siren's summons and had taken the place aft that the second mate should rightfully have occupied had he been on the ship.

For hundreds of years, since the first sailors sailed the sea, it has been the custom to repeat orders. It prevents mistakes. It was adopted for that reason. There can be no mistakes at sea. The sea itself watches out for that.

So Mr. Murphy shouted back, repeating the command, "Let go aft, sir! Hold her with the spring!" And automatically checking the order in his mind, the captain mumbled "Aye, aye" as he went to the for'ard dodger and shouted to the mate.

A jangle of telegraphs, and the engine commenced pulsing like a great heart. Slowly the ship moved. The stevedores on the wharf gaped as tho they had never seen a ship move before. A few loafers spat tobacco into the bay from where they sat on the piles and registered interest. Three men ran from bollard to bollard and threw off hawsers as the ship's officers directed.

"Starboard a bit!" the captain called deeply.

Shorty sniffed as he turned the wheel. "Starboard a bit," he said. His little eyes were intent on the quadrant before him where a tell-tale registered the movements of the rudder. He checked the wheel when the tell-tale had gone far enough.

The ship's bow edged out from the wharf.

"Slack away for'ard!" shouted the captain. The mate repeated the order. Then he yelled to the seaman who was holding the turns of the only hawser still fast to the wharf, the breast-rope, on the windlass drum.

The man "surged," that is, let a little of the hawser slide through his hands. The steam hissed as the drum, relieved momentarily of the strain, clanked round a turn or two. The carpenter, at the throttle, shut off the steam altogether and the drum stopped. The seaman slacked still further, watching the mate.

The wire spring, the only rope now out astern, began

to slacken as the after end of the ship came in and
rubbed along the wharf. Slowly the bows cleared the
stern of the steam schooner ahead whose captain was
leaning over the bridge-rail and hungrily watching that
no damage was done to his vessel.

The telegraphs jangled again. The engines stopped.

"Slack away aft!" called the captain. He was handi-
capped, being on the bridge by himself. When he had
all officers on board, the third mate was supposed to
stand by the telegraphs and to repeat orders to the
helmsman. That prevented the captain running all over
the bridge and enabled him to give his fixed attention
to plotting his next move.

As it was, he peered first for'ard, gaging distances,
anxiously eyeing the rip of the outgoing tide, watching
the nearing sand-bank on his port bow. Again he paced
aft and peered to see his ship's stern was not being
chafed too much against the wharf-piling. He measured
the force of the wind, trying to estimate just how
much it would start the ship drifting. Back again he
swung, fearful lest he should smash into the stern of
the steam schooner and incur a damage suit. He was
worried about the water. Was there enough to float
his ship? The tide was still falling.

"Let go for'ard!" he shouted suddenly. The mate
yelled the order to the seaman at the windlass. The
man hastily flung off two of the three turns of the
hawser he had round the drum. Another seaman as
hastily flung clear several bights of the hawser from the
great coil against the ship's rail. When there was only
one turn on the drum, the seaman "laid back" on the
rope and let it run quickly through his fingers till all
strain was gone and the hawser sagged to the deck of
the fo'c'sle-head and again to the water beyond the ship.

Then the seaman flung off the last turn and stood clear while the hawser slicked out through the fair-leads, slower and slower, and finally ceased moving.

"Let go ashore!" yelled the mate, standing on the fair-leads and holding to the rail with one hand. The three stevedores casting off lines from the bollards waved and raced for the eye of the slack hawser. They heaved up on it and slipped it clear. It fell with a tremendous splash into the dull swirling waters.

"Pick up yer slack!" yelled the mate, twisting his head to the windlass. The two seamen handling the hawser jumped for the thick rope and, lifting it, took a couple of turns round the windlass drum as the bos'n, coiling up a heaving line, repeated the order.

"Let 'er buck, chips!" called one of the seamen to the carpenter. That worthy turned the throttle and the windlass clanked and raced, the drum rolled around and the hawser came dripping up through the fair-leads, slimy with bay mud. One seaman took it hand-over-hand off the racing drum. The other seaman coiled it profanely on top of the coils that had not been used so far and were dry but for the dampening drizzle.

"All gone for'ard, sir!" cried the mate, stepping back on to the deck from the fair-leads and facing the bridge.

"Aye, aye," responded the captain. Hastily he faced aft. The ship was now moving away and ahead from the wharf at an angle of about forty-five degrees. Anxiously the captain eyed the swirling water overside. His face was drawn with the tension of responsibility. How fast was the water running?

"Let go aft!" he shouted suddenly. The third mate echoed the order.

The seaman holding the double wire round the starboard winch drum "surged," or slacked, away. The wire kinked behind him and the third mate himself cleared it. The telegraphs jangled on the bridge, "Half ahead." The engine started beating like a great heart again. The ship moved.

Her bow was now well past the stern of the steam schooner. On the wharf the three stevedores stood by the after bollard and waited for the wire to slack so that they could throw the bight clear. The after winch rattled. The wire had jammed, one turn over another, and the third mate was trying to clear it by backing up with the drum. It was bad wire, old and cheap. It kinked very easily. The delay allowed the ship to get ahead of the slack. The wire tautened, sang with the tension.

The third mate swore viciously. The seaman holding the slack end of the wire grew nervous. In some way the turns were twisted so that they would not clear readily.

"Hold on!" the officer shouted hastily to the bridge. The captain spun on his heel to see what was the matter. He jumped for the telegraph.

Whang! went the wire as it parted. It broke between ship and wharf. It curled back like a vicious snake, smashed against the poop-rail. A great kink caught in the fair-leads. The third mate reversed the winch desperately to see if, now the wire had gone, he could not snatch it inboard and clear the twisted turns. He didn't know the kink was in the fair-leads. The winch drum strained. There was another whang! The wire between the winch and the rail broke, the frayed end curled over, like a spring, and smashed the seaman at the drum across the chest. He went over backwards with a cry. He rolled on the deck and moaned. Blood came from his mouth. The third mate sprang to him, shutting off the winch steam.

"All gone aft, sir!" he shouted, white-faced, as he bent down. The captain, aware that something had happened, faced the bows. He desperately wanted to see what was wrong aft. He knew, whatever it was, he could straighten it out with a few cool orders. But the third mate was a youngster, not used to handling a watch when shifting ship. Lines appeared on the captain's brow. He grew uneasy. But he daren't pay too much attention astern. His ship was swinging free in the river. A steam schooner crowded her on the starboard beam, a sand-bank on the port. Two hundred feet wide was the channel. The fate of thousands of dollars' worth of property, lives, his own job, hung between his lips.

Oh, what *was* the water depth? And how fast was the tide running? Was it fast enough to affect the ship? And the wind? Why couldn't the fool agent wait?

The tide rips caught the ship as she swung clear of the steam schooner. She started to swing rapidly, bow on to the sand-bank.

"Hard a-port!" shouted the captain. Shorty at the wheel repeated the command quite unperturbed. It didn't matter to *him* if the ship sank even.

"Full ahead!" rang the telegraphs; came their answering jangle. The captain ran to the starboard side of the bridge and eyed the steam schooner. Would his stern clear?

On the fo'c'sle-head the mate anxiously watched the nearing sand-bank.

The ship still swung, the screw being slow to take up power. Her stern grazed the stern of the steam schooner. But the steam schooner's captain already had a man holding a cork fender overside at the point of contact. There was a shuddering rasp. Came the point of strain for the stout man on the bridge.

"Blankety-blankety-blank-blank-blank!" yelled the steam schooner captain. "Get that barge of yours away from my ship!"

An old bay seaman shouted from the wharf, "Look out for shoal-water, skipper."

"Ten fathoms' clearance yet, sir!" called the mate from the cat-heads for'ard. He was speaking of the sand-bank.

"My God, get a doctor!" the third mate was crying hysterically from aft.

The captain's jaw tightened. The little muscles stood out near his ears. He thrust his hands into his side pockets and kept his gaze fixed rigidly ahead. His eyes wore a bleak, cold look. He seemed to be listening for a message that came from far away. His head was inclined slightly to the wind. Watching him then, you could understand why he was one of the most reliable sailors on that wild coast.

It was a matter of chance and moments whether the ship would answer her helm before she hit the sand-bank. Or she might ground in the very channel. If she had not enough power to breast the rips at all, she might sweep far out into the bay, her swiftly let-go anchors dragging up the mud.

"Ease the helm," said the captain at last, suddenly, evenly. The helm was beginning to answer. Scarce six fathoms, thirty-six feet, separated the bow from the edge of the bank.

Shorty in the wheel-house spat aside calmly. "Ease the helm," he said. Looking aft for a brief moment, the captain saw a group of men carrying an inert form towards the saloon. He noted the third mate had had sense enough not to leave his post.

There was a hoarse whistle on the port beam. The captain twisted abruptly and saw a little ferry-boat breasting the rips and crowding for the scant channel between the ship's bow and the sand-bank. The ferry whistled again. Like a nervous woman screaming, the captain thought grimly. He took no notice.

The ferry captain shouted frantically. The few passengers on the little craft's upper deck shouted. Again the whistle screamed. The captain stared ahead and said nothing. His ship was swinging clear. To the other captain his own vessel.

The mate on the fo'c'sle-head sighed as the sand-bank started to recede. "Close," he mumbled.

"Good heavens," said the tall agent on the lower bridge, sneeringly watching all things, "the captain is the most careless man I ever saw. Takes a lot of time to shift a small ship a hundred yards."

"Good man, Cap'n Roscoe," commented the old bay-sailor who had shouted from the wharf about shoal-water. "Notice he knows what he's doing?"

"You're all right now," sang out the captain of the steam schooner good-naturedly as he waved his hand. "Waters pretty shallow just off my beam, tho."

The captain on the ship's bridge merely nodded and lifted a hand in greeting. It seemed neither man remembered the language the one had used not five minutes previously.

The ferry shot under the ship's bows still screaming with her whistle. Her passengers had quit shouting, there being nothing now to shout for. For a minute they had expected to get caught between the ship and the sand-bank. Strain had overwhelmed them.

Said the mate, a little testily, "Bos'n, get a line ready to send ashore."

"Aye, aye, sir," called the bos'n, and he stooped and bent a heaving line on to the spliced eye of a great eight-inch hawser.

"Port a bit more," said the captain evenly. Shorty mumbled the order, for he was taking a fresh chew of tobacco, and spun the wheel with one hand.

On the wharf the second mate of the ship, just hurriedly arrived from uptown, stood and anxiously watched proceedings. He wondered whether he would get called down by the captain for not being on hand to shift ship. He noticed a broken wire dangling from the after-leads and swore. He supposed some other man had taken his place and made a mess of things. He was alternately sulky and apprehensive.

Parallel now with the steam schooner the ship slid. Her speed was very slow because of the rips. The wind caught her and veered her dangerously close to the schooner's side. The captain spoke to the helmsman, the wheel turned quickly, the error was corrected.

There was a slight bump and the ship went still slower, threatening to stop. The captain peered to port and starboard. The screw threshed evenly. Mud and water boiled on the surface. A foul smell tainted the air.

"Stop," rang the telegraphs. The captain shouted for'ard.

"Take a cast, Mr. Leach!"

"Aye, aye, sir," said the mate, and he spoke to the bos'n, who took the matter in hand personally and swung the sounding-lead. The depth was shouted.

"Ought to make it," the captain muttered. "Full astern," jangled the telegraphs. The ship moved back, jerkily. Shorty was kept busy at the wheel holding the bow straight against rips and the wind.

"Full ahead," went the telegraphs. The ship jerked forward. She struck the mud once more, hesitated a bit, and then plowed slowly on. Her keel furrowed several inches in the bay-floor. But the obstruction was only a narrow ridge. And the ship was half over already. Deep water was a fathom or so away. So the lead said and the lead never lied.

"Get a line ashore, Mr. Leach!" called the captain, for now the ship was past the steam schooner, over the ridge of mud and sand.

"Line ashore, sir," shouted back the mate, and he spoke to the bos'n, who was coiling away the hand-lead. The bos'n spoke to a seaman and the man picked up a heaving-line and waited.

"Port a bit!" said the captain, and Shorty in the wheel-house below responded. The ship's bow swung slightly towards number three wharf.

The three stevedores who had shifted the lines on the other wharf waited the incoming ship. The marooned second mate waited. The old bay-seaman watched with critical eyes how the ship was handled.

"Get a line ashore aft!" shouted the captain.

"Line ashore aft, sir," the third mate acknowledged. He picked up a heaving-line himself and coiled it. He wondered as he did so how the injured seaman was getting on.

The seaman on the fo'c'sle-head cast his line. It fell short. He coiled it in, hand-over-hand, and cast again. One of the stevedores on the wharf puts his foot hastily on the "monkey's knot" on the end before it could slip back into the water. It was hauled ashore. The bight of the hawser followed.

The third mate cast from aft and another stevedore caught his line. Another hawser was hauled ashore.

"Starboard a bit," said Shorty as he spun the wheel. The ship straightened out. She was parallel with the wharf, her stern about five fathoms from the steam schooner's bow. The tide-rips eased up as slack water approached. The wind could do only good now, blowing the ship on to her berth.

"Slow," rang the engine-room telegraphs under the captain's hand.

"Good work!" muttered the old seaman on the wharf.

"My God, he's slow!" grumbled the tweed-clad agent on the lower bridge, impatiently fingering his watch-chain.

"Take in your slack!" called the captain, first for'ard and then aft. Twice the repeated call came to him. He nodded and walked across the bridge to look at the wharf.

"Some fenders midships, Mr. Leach!" he called. The mate waved his hand. He spoke to the bos'n, who spoke to a seaman. The man hurried below under the fo'c'sle-head, and appeared after a while staggering under three cork fenders. These he tied by their lanyards to the rail midships so that the actual fender-ball hung well down the ship's side and would ward off direct impact with the nearing wharf.

"Vast heaving for'ard!" said the captain.

"Vast heaving," replied the mate. He held up his hand and the seaman holding the rope on the windlass-drum "surged" a little but still kept the strain.

"Heave away aft!" the captain shouted. The third

mate repeated and quickened the speed of the winch-
drum so that the hawser came in faster. The ship had
been slipping off the parallel again. Now she straightened out once more as the after hawser slicked in.

"Heave away for'ard!" said the captain. The mate
called back and the windlass resumed its clanking hiss.

"Stop," rang the telegraphs. The answering jangle
mingled with the captain's shout, "Get a spring out
aft!"

"Get a spring out, sir," responded the third mate.
Leaving a seaman to haul away on the hawser, he took
one man and uncoiled another wire from a reel, snaking
it along the deck ready for running. Another heaving-
line was brought and attached to the bight of the wire.

"Easy," the mate said to his men. The windlass
turned slower. The ship was well-nigh on the wharf.

"Slow astern," went the engine-room telegraphs, for
the ship was sliding ahead too much.

"Shift your line for'ard a bit!" roared the captain to
the third mate. The third mate shouted to the stevedores on the wharf and then snapped a command back
at the winch-crew. The hawser was "surged," drooped,
slacked right off, and the stevedores on the wharf lifted
the bight from the bollard it was on and carried it
farther for'ard.

"Stop," rang the telegraphs noisily. Then, "Finished
with Engines."

"Make fast fore and aft!" shouted the captain.

"Make fast, sir," the mate and the third called back.
A wire spring was got out for'ard. Another hawser
served as a breast rope. Two more ropes went aft.
After a while, "All fast, sir," came from aft. "All fast,
sir," came from for'ard.

S. S. VIII-3

"Swing the derricks out, Mr. Leach," said the captain, leaning over the bridge-rail.

"Aye, aye, sir. Swing the derricks out," said the mate.

"Get the gangway overside, Mr. Murphy!" called the captain to the young officer aft.

"The gangway? Aye, aye, sir," returned the third mate. He finished taking turns with the hawsers round the bitts. He watched a seaman frap a seizing of marlin round double wire where it was on the bitts near the mainmast, and then he took two men to where the gangway rested on number three hatch.

The captain grunted, took his hands from his side pockets, and filled his pipe. As he struck a match and lit it, he paused by the chart-house.

"That'll do the wheel!" he called to the helmsman. Shorty grunted, spat tobacco-juice aside, and looked up.

"That'll do the wheel!" he called to the helmsman. put his helm amidships, swinging the spokes till the brass tell-tale of the quadrant ran straight fore and aft. Then he stepped off the grating and made his way for'ard.

The derrick-booms swung overside. Guys were slackened and tautened. Stevedores swarmed aboard. The captain came down from the navigation-bridge and made his way to his room. He flung himself into a chair and sighed.

"Damn fool," he said at last to the inkwell. Then he removed his uniform-cap and laid it on his desk. He took up his pen and went on writing his unfinished letter.

"Say, captain, d'you know it's taken you nearly an hour to shift? My Gawd, you're so slow! You forget about docking-dues and all that. I . . ."

"Oh, yes," said the captain wearily as he laid down his pen and looked up into the agent's sour face. "I suppose I did take a long time. There were many things to be considered. But I wish you'd leave me run my ship in my own way."

"Telegram, sir," said the steward, pushing contemptuously by the agent in the doorway and approaching the captain. "Just came."

"Thanks." The captain took the telegram. "And, by the way, steward!" The white-jacketed steward paused.

"Yes, sir?" he said.

The captain frowned. "Was anyone hurt aft when that wire broke?"

The steward grinned.

"No, sir. A sailor got a crack in the chest, but the doctor says he'll be all right in a day or so."

"I see. Ah, you might send the third mate to me."

"The third mate? Yes, sir. At once, sir." The steward pushed past the agent again and vanished. The captain slit open the telegram and scanned the message it contained. His eyes twinkled. He even laughed a little.

"I'll report this to the owners," nagged the agent, waving his hand in the air. "I suppose there'll be a damage suit for scraping that blasted steam schooner's stern. Why don't you be more careful? I can't understand . . ."

"Oh, shut up!" growled the captain, looking up, his smile disappearing. "Shut up, for heaven's sake! Do you think I scrape other ships on purpose? I told you it was awkward to handle a craft right now. I did my best and the ship's safe. Go away and leave me in peace."

"That's all right to talk. What about the time you took? I tell you Jack Esmer of the *Wallaby* shifted his ship in half an hour last Wednesday."

The captain rose to his feet.

"Maybe," he said. "I happen to know he shifted at high tide and on a fine day. Now don't you stand there and try to tell me my business. I've spent thirty years at sea learning it. See this wire?"

He held out the telegram he had received and the agent took it with a scowl.

"It says," went on the captain, "that I've got five thousand dollars coming to me as salvage-money on the towing of the *Nonet* to safety last year. It's just been awarded. The case has been in court for twelve months. . . . Now do you know what that five thousand dollars means to me?"

"No. Can't say I do. Anyway . . ." The agent made to hand the telegram back.

"Shut up!" roared the captain. "I'll tell you what it means! It means that I can be independent of scum like you! It means that I can smash you on the nose and get fired and still laugh, see? Well, take it!"

His great fist swung viciously up and the agent sat down on the deck outside the cabin with remarkable suddenness.

"Oh!" he gurgled. "Oh!"

"And if you want any more, stand up," grunted the captain. Then he went inside the cabin and slammed the door shut.

"What's the matter?" asked the third mate of the groaning tweed-clad figure as he came along the deck a few moments later. But the agent did not answer. He only glared.

The third mate grinned as he knocked on the door

of the captain's cabin. He went in as a deep voice
called an invitation. Weakly the agent rose to his feet
and staggered away.

"Oh!" he groaned again. "Oh!"

"This way," said the mate firmly, as he caught the
agent's arm on the main-deck and guided the man to
the gangway. He had seen the captain's blow from
where he had stood by number two hatch. He was
pleased. While he did not dare to insult the agent, he
could make his feelings plain. He gave the agent a
sharp push when he was started down the shallow
steps.

"Good-by, sir." The mate chuckled. "Hope you
come again." But the agent, fondling his face, had only
time to get home and to a mirror at the earliest possible moment, and to grope through his astonished
mind for a reason for what had occurred.

THE OUTLAWS

By Selma Lagerlof

A peasant had killed a monk and fled to the woods.
He became an outlaw, upon whose head a price was set.
In the forest he met another fugitive, a young fisherman from one of the outermost islands, who had been
accused of the theft of a herring net. The two became
companions, cut themselves a home in a cave, laid their
nets together, cooked their food, made their arrows,
and held watch one for the other. The peasant could
never leave the forest. But the fisherman, whose crime
was less serious, would now and then take upon his back
the game they had killed, and would creep down to the
more isolated houses on the outskirts of the village. In
return for milk, butter, arrow-heads, and clothing he
would sell his game, the black mountain cock, the
moor hen, with her shining feathers, the toothsome doe,
and the long-eared hare.

The cave which was their home cut down deep into a
mountain-side. The entrance was guarded by wide
slabs of stone and ragged thorn-bushes. High up on
the hillside there stood a giant pine, and the chimney
of the fireplace nestled among its coiled roots. Thus
the smoke could draw up through the heavy hanging
branches and fade unseen into the air. To reach their
cave the men had to wade through the stream that
sprang out from the hill slope. No pursuer thought of

seeking their trail in this merry brooklet. At first they were hunted as wild animals are. The peasants of the district gathered to pursue them as if for a baiting of wolf or bear. The bowmen surrrounded the wood while the spear carriers entered and left no thicket or ravine unsearched. The two outlaws cowered in their gloomy cave, panting in terror and listening breathlessly as the hunt passed on with noise and shouting over the mountain ranges.

For one long day the young fisherman lay motionless, but the murderer could stand it no longer, and went out into the open where he could see his enemy. They discovered him and set after him, but this was far more to his liking than lying quiet in impotent terror. He fled before his pursuers, leaped the streams, slid down the precipices, climbed up perpendicular walls of rock. All his remarkable strength and skill awoke to energy under the spur of danger. His body became as elastic as a steel spring, his foot held firm, his hand grasped sure, his eye and ear were doubly sharp. He knew the meaning of every murmur in the foliage; he could understand the warning in an upturned stone.

When he had clambered up the side of a precipice he would stop to look down on his pursuers, greeting them with loud songs of scorn. When their spears sang above him in the air, he would catch them and hurl them back. As he crashed his way through tangled underbrush something within him seemed to sing a wild song of rejoicing. A gaunt, bare hilltop stretched itself through the forest, and all alone upon its crest there stood a towering pine. The red brown trunk was bare, in the thick grown boughs at the top a hawk's nest rocked in the breeze. So daring had the fugitive grown that on another day he climbed to the nest while his

pursuers sought him in the woody slopes below. He
sat there and twisted the necks of the young hawks as
the hunt raged far beneath him. The old birds flew
screaming about him in anger. They swooped past his
face, they struck at his eyes with their beaks, beat at
him with their powerful wings, and clawed great
scratches in his weather-hardened skin. He battled
with them laughing. He stood up in the rocking nest
as he lunged at the birds with his knife, and he lost all
thought of danger and pursuit in the joy of the battle.
When recollection came again and he turned to look
for his enemies, the hunt had gone off in another direction. Not one of the pursuers had thought of raising
his eyes to the clouds to see the prey hanging there,
doing schoolboy deeds of recklessness while his life
hung in the balance. But the man trembled from head
to foot when he saw that he was safe. He caught for
a support with his shaking hands; he looked down
giddily from the height to which he had climbed.
Groaning in fear of a fall, afraid of the birds, afraid
of the possibility of being seen, weakened through terror of everything and anything, he slid back down the
tree trunk. He laid himself flat upon the earth and
crawled over the loose stones until he reached the
underbrush. There he hid among the tangled branches
of the young pines, sinking down, weak and helpless,
upon the soft moss. A single man might have captured
him.

. . . .

Tord was the name of the fisherman. He was but
sixteen years old, but was strong and brave. He had
now lived for a whole year in the wood.

The peasant's name was Berg, and they had called

him "The Giant." He was handsome and well-built,
the tallest and strongest man in the entire county. He
was broad-shouldered and yet slender. His hands were
delicate in shape, as if they had never known hard
work, his hair was brown, his face soft-colored. When
he had lived for some time in the forest his look of
strength was awe-inspiring. His eyes grew piercing
under bushy brows wrinkled by great muscles over the
forehead. His lips were more firmly set than before,
his face more haggard, with deepened hollows at the
temples, and his strongly marked cheek-bones stood out
plainly. All the softer curves of his body disappeared,
but the muscles grew strong as steel. His hair turned
gray rapidly.

Tord had never seen any one so magnificent and so
mighty before. In his imagination, his companion
towered high as the forest, strong as the raging surf.
He served him humbly, as he would have served a
master, he revered him as he would have revered a
god. It seemed quite natural that Tord should carry
the hunting spear, that he should drag the game home,
draw the water, and build the fire. Berg, the Giant,
accepted all these services, but scarce threw the boy a
friendly word. He looked upon him with contempt, as
a common thief.

The outlaws did not live by pillage, but supported
themselves by hunting and fishing. Had not Berg killed
a holy man, the peasants would soon have tired of the
pursuit and left them to themselves in the mountains.
But they feared disaster for the villages if he who had
laid hands upon a servant of God should go unpunished.
When Tord took his game down into the valley they
would offer him money and a pardon for himself if he
would lead them to the cave of the Giant, that they

might catch the latter in his sleep. But the boy refused, and if they followed him he would lead them astray until they gave up the pursuit.

Once Berg asked him whether the peasants had ever tried to persuade him to betrayal. When he learned what reward they had promised he said scornfully that Tord was a fool not to accept such offers. Tord looked at him with something in his eyes that Berg, the Giant, had never seen before. No beautiful woman whom he had loved in the days of his youth had ever looked at him like that; not even in the eyes of his own children, or of his wife, had he seen such affection. "You are my God, the ruler I have chosen of my own free will." This was what the eyes said. "You may scorn me, or beat me, if you will, but I shall still remain faithful."

From this on Berg gave more heed to the boy and saw that he was brave in action but shy in speech. Death seemed to have no terrors for him. He would deliberately choose for his path the fresh formed ice on the mountain pools, the treacherous surface of the morass in springtime. He seemed to delight in danger. It gave him some compensation for the wild ocean storms he could no longer go out to meet. He would tremble in the night darkness of the wood, however, and even by day the gloom of a thicket or a deeper shadow could frighten him. When Berg asked him about this he was silent in embarrassment.

Tord did not sleep in the bed by the hearth at the back of the cave, but every night, when Berg was asleep the boy would creep to the entrance and lie there on one of the broad stones. Berg discovered this, and altho he guessed the reason he asked the boy about it. Tord would not answer. To avoid further questions he slept in the bed for two nights, then returned to his post at the door.

One night, when a snow-storm raged in the tree-tops, piling up drifts even in the heart of the thickets, the flakes swirled into the cave of the outlaws. Tord, lying by the entrance, awoke in the morning to find himself wrapped in a blanket of melting snow. A day or two later he fell ill. Sharp pains pierced his lungs when he tried to draw breath. He endured the pain as long as his strength would stand it, but one evening, when he stooped to blow up the fire, he fell down and could not rise again. Berg came to his side and told him to lie in the warm bed. Tord groaned in agony, but could not move. Berg put his arm under the boy's body and carried him to the bed. He had a feeling while doing it as if he were touching a clammy snake; he had a taste in his mouth as if he had eaten unclean horse-flesh, so repulsive was it to him to touch the person of this common thief. Berg covered the sick boy with his own warm bear-skin rug and gave him water. This was all he could do, but the illness was not dangerous, and Tord recovered quickly. But now that Berg had had to do his companion's work for a few days and had had to care for him, they seemed to have come nearer to one another. Tord dared to speak to Berg sometimes, as they sat together by the fire cutting their arrows.

"You come of good people, Berg," Tord said one evening. "Your relatives are the richest peasants in the valley. The men of your name have served kings and fought in their castles."

"They have more often fought with the rebels and done damage to the king's property," answered Berg.

"Your forefathers held great banquets at Christmas

time. And you held banquets too, when you were at home in your house. Hundreds of men and women could find place on the benches in your great hall, the hall that was built in the days before St. Olaf came here to Viken for christening. Great silver urns were there, and mighty horns, filled with mead, went the rounds of your table."

Berg looked at the boy again. He sat on the edge of the bed with his head in his hands, pushing back the heavy tangled hair that hung over his eyes. His face had become pale and refined through his illness. His eyes still sparkled in fever. He smiled to himself at the pictures called up by his fancy—pictures of the great hall and of the silver urns, of the richly clad guests, and of Berg, the Giant, lording it in the place of honor. The peasant knew that even in the days of his glory no one had ever looked at him with eyes so shining in admiration, so glowing in reverence, as this boy did now, as he sat by the fire in his worn leather jacket. He was touched, and yet displeased. This common thief had no right to admire him.

"Were there no banquets in your home?" he asked.

Tord laughed: "Out there on the rocks where father and mother live? Father plunders the wrecks and mother is a witch. When the weather is stormy she rides out to meet the ships on a seal's back, and those who are washed overboard from the wrecks belong to her."

"What does she do with them?" asked Berg.

"Oh, a witch always needs corpses. She makes salves of them, or perhaps she eats them. On moonlit nights she sits out in the wildest surf and looks for the eyes and fingers of drowned children."

"That is horrible!" said Berg.

The boy answered with calm confidence: "It would be for others, but not for a witch. She can't help it."

This was an altogether new manner of looking at life for Berg. "Then thieves have to steal, as witches have to make magic?" he questioned sharply.

"Why, yes," answered the boy. "Every one has to do the thing he was born for." But a smile of shy cunning curled his lips, as he added: "There are thieves who have never stolen."

"What do you mean by that?" spoke Berg.

The boy still smiled his mysterious smile and seemed happy to have given his companion a riddle. "There are birds that do not fly; and there are thieves who have not stolen," he said.

Berg feigned stupidity, in order to trick the other's meaning: "How can any one be called a thief who has never stolen?" he said.

The boy's lips closed tight as if to hold back the words. "But if one has a father who steals—" he threw out after a short pause.

"A man may inherit house and money, but the name thief is given only to him who earns it."

Tord laughed gently. "But when one has a mother —and that mother comes and cries, and begs one to take upon one's self the father's crime—and then one can laugh at the hangman and run away into the woods. A man may be outlawed for the sake of a fish net he has never seen."

Berg beat his fist upon the stone table, in great anger. Here this strong, beautiful boy had thrown away his whole life for another. Neither love, nor riches, nor the respect of his fellow men could ever be his again. The sordid care for food and clothing was all that remained to him in life. And this fool had let him,

Berg, despise an innocent man. He scolded sternly, but
Tord was not frightened any more than a sick child is
frightened at the scolding of his anxious mother.

.   .   .   .

High up on one of the broad wooded hills there lay
a black swampy lake. It was square in shape, and its
banks were as straight, and their corners as sharp as if
it had been the work of human hands. On three sides
steep walls of rock rose up, with hardy mountain pines
clinging to the stones, their roots as thick as a man's
arm. At the surface of the lake, where the few strips
of grass had been washed away, these naked roots
twisted and coiled, rising out of the water like myriad
snakes that had tried to escape from the waves, but
had been turned to stone in their struggle. Or was it
more like a mass of blackened skeletons of long-
drowned giants which the lake was trying to throw off?
The arms and legs were twisted in wild contortions, the
long fingers grasped deep into the rocks, the mighty
ribs formed arches that upheld ancient trees. But now
and again these iron-hard arms, these steel fingers with
which the climbing pines supported themselves, would
loosen their hold, and then the strong north wind would
hurl the tree from the ridge far out into the swamp.
There it would lie, its crown burrowing deep in the
muddy water. The fishes found good hiding places
amid its twigs, while the roots rose up over the water
like the arms of some hideous monster, giving the little
lake a repulsive appearance.

The mountains sloped down on the fourth side of the
little lake. A tiny rivulet foamed out here; but before
the stream could find its path it twisted and turned
among boulders and mounds of earth, forming a whole

colony of islands, some of which scarce offered foot-
hold, while others carried as many as twenty trees on
their back.

Here, where the rocks were not high enough to shut
out the sun, the lighter foliaged trees could grow.
Here were the timid, gray-green alders, and the willows
with their smooth leaves. Birches were here, as they
always are wherever there is a chance to shut out the
evergreens, and there were mountain ash and elder
bushes, giving charm and fragrance to the place.

At the entrance to the lake there was a forest of
rushes as high as a man's head, through which the sun-
light fell as green upon the water as it falls on the
moss in the true forest. There were little clearings
among the reeds, little round ponds where the water-
lilies slumbered. The tall rushes looked down with
gentle gravity upon these sensitive beauties, who closed
their white leaves and their yellow hearts so quickly in
their leather outer dress as soon as the sun withdrew
his rays.

One sunny day the outlaws came to one of these little
ponds to fish. They waded through the reeds to two
high stones, and sat there throwing out their bait for
the big green, gleaming pike that slumbered just below
the surface of the water. These men, whose life was
now passed entirely among the mountains and the
woods, had come to be as completely under the control
of the powers of nature as were the plants or the animals. When the sun shone they were open-hearted and
merry, at evening they became silent, and the night,
which seemed to them so all-powerful, robbed them of
their strength. And now the green light that fell
through the reeds and drew out from the water stripes
of gold, brown, and black-green, smoothed them into a

sort of magic mood. They were completely shut out
from the outer world. The reeds swayed gently in the
soft wind, the rushes murmured, and the long, ribbon-
like leaves struck them lightly in the face. They sat
on the gray stones in their gray leather garments, and
the shaded tones of the leather melted into the shades
of the stones. Each saw his comrade sitting opposite
him as quietly as a stone statue. And among the reeds
they saw giant fish swimming, gleaming and glittering
in all colors of the rainbow. When the men threw out
their lines and watched the rings on the water widen
amid the reeds, it seemed to them that the motion grew
and grew until they saw it was not they themselves
alone that had occasioned it. A Nixie, half human, half
fish, lay sleeping deep down in the water. She lay on
her back, and the waves clung so closely to her body
that the men had not seen her before. It was her
breath that stirred the surface. But it did not seem to
the watchers that there was anything strange in the
fact that she lay there. And when she had disappeared
in the next moment they did not know whether her
appearance had been an illusion or not.

The green light pierced through their eyes into their
brains like a mild intoxication. They saw visions among
the reeds, visions which they would not tell even to
each other. There was not much fishing done. The
day was given up to dreams and visions.

A sound of oars came from among the reeds, and
they started up out of their dreaming. In a few moments a heavy boat, hewn out of a tree trunk, came
into sight, set in motion by oars not much broader than
walking sticks. The oars were in the hands of a young
girl who had been gathering water-lilies. She had long,
dark brown braids of hair, and great dark eyes, but she

was strangely pale, a pallor that was not gray, but
softly pink tinted. Her cheeks were no deeper in color
than the rest of her face; her lips were scarce redder.
She wore a bodice of white linen and a leather belt
with a golden clasp. Her skirt was of blue with a
broad red hem. She rowed past close by the outlaws
without seeing them. They sat absolutely quiet, less
from fear of discovery than from the desire to look at
her undisturbed. When she had gone, the stone statues
became men again and smiled:

"She was as white as the water-lilies," said one.
"And her eyes were as dark as the water back there
under the roots of the pines."

They were both so merry that they felt like laughing,
like really laughing as they had never laughed in this
swamp before, a laugh that would echo back from the
wall of rock and loosen the roots of the pines.

"Did you think her beautiful?" asked the Giant.

"I do not know, she passed so quickly. Perhaps she
was beautiful."

"You probably did not dare to look at her. Did you
think she was the Nixie?"

And again they felt a strange desire to laugh.

. . . .

While a child, Tord had once seen a drowned man.
He had found the corpse on the beach in broad day-
light, and it had not frightened him, but at night his
dreams were terrifying. He had seemed to be looking
out over an ocean, every wave of which threw a dead
body at his feet. He saw all the rocks and islands
covered with corpses of the drowned, the drowned that
were dead and belonged to the sea, but that could move,

and speak, and threaten him with their white stiffened fingers.

And so it was again. The girl whom he had seen in the reeds appeared to him in his dreams. He met her again down at the bottom of the swamp lake, where the light was greener even than in the reeds, and there he had time enough to see that she was beautiful. He dreamed that he sat on one of the great pine roots in the midst of the lake while the tree rocked up and down, now under, now over the surface of the water. Then he saw her on one of the smallest islands. She stood under the red mountain ash and laughed at him. In his very last dream it had gone so far that she had kissed him. But then it was morning, and he heard Berg rising, but he kept his eyes stubbornly closed that he might continue to dream. When he did awake he was dazed and giddy from what he had seen during the night. He thought much more about the girl than he had done the day before. Toward evening it occurred to him to ask Berg if he knew her name.

Berg looked at him sharply. "It is better for you to know it at once," he said. "It was Unn. We are related to each other."

And then Tord knew that it was this pale maiden who was the cause of Berg's wild hunted life in forest and mountain. He tried to search his memory for what he had heard about her.

Unn was the daughter of a free peasant. Her mother was dead, and she ruled in her father's household. This was to her taste, for she was independent by nature, and had no inclination to give herself to any husband. Unn and Berg were cousins, and the rumor had long gone about that Berg liked better to sit with Unn and her maids than to work at home in his own house. One

Christmas, when the great banquet was to be given in
Berg's hall, his wife had invited a monk from Draks-
mark, who, she hoped, would show Berg how wrong it
was that he should neglect her for another. Berg and
others besides him hated this monk because of his appearance. He was very stout and absolutely white.
The ring of hair around his bald head, the brows above
his moist eyes, the color of his skin, of his hands, and
of his garments, were all white. Many found him very
repulsive to look at.

But the monk was fearless, and as he believed that
his words would have greater weight if many heard
them, he rose at the table before all the guests, and
said: "Men call the cuckoo the vilest of birds because
he brings up his young in the nest of others. But here
sits a man who takes no care for his house and his children, and who seeks his pleasure with a strange woman.
Him I will call the vilest of men." Unn rose in her
place. "Berg, this is said to you and to me," she cried.
"Never have I been so shamed, but my father is not
here to protect me." She turned to go, but Berg
hurried after her. "Stay where you are," she said. "I
do not wish to see you again." He stopped her in the
corridor, and asked her what he should do that she
might stay with him. Her eyes glowed as she answered
that he himself should know best what he must do.
Then Berg went into the hall again and slew the monk.

Berg and Tord thought on awhile with the same
thoughts, then Berg said: "You should have seen her
when the white monk fell. My wife drew the children
about her and cursed Unn. She turned the faces of
the children toward her, that they might always remember the woman for whose sake their father had
become a murderer. But Unn stood there so quiet and

so beautiful that the men who saw her trembled. She thanked me for the deed, and prayed me to flee to the woods at once. She told me never to become a robber, and to use my knife only in some cause equally just."

"Your deed had ennobled her," said Tord.

And again Berg found himself astonished at the same thing that had before now surprized him in the boy. Tord was a heathen, or worse than a heathen; he never condemned that which was wrong. He seemed to know no sense of responsibility. What had to come, came. He knew of God, of Christ, and the Saints, but he knew them only by name, as one knows the names of the gods of other nations. The ghosts of the Scheeren Islands were his gods. His mother, learned in magic, had taught him to believe in the spirits of the dead. And then it was that Berg undertook a task which was as foolish as if he had woven a rope for his own neck. He opened the eyes of this ignorant boy to the power of God, the Lord of all Justice, the avenger of wrong, who condemned sinners to the pangs of hell everlasting. And he taught him to love Christ and His Mother, and all the saintly men and women who sit before the throne of God praying that His anger may be turned away from sinners. He taught him all that mankind has learned to do to soften the wrath of God. He told him of the long trains of pilgrims journeying to the holy places; he told him of those who scourged themselves in their remorse; and he told him of the pious monks who flee the joys of this world.

The longer he spoke the paler grew the boy and the keener his attention as his eyes widened at the visions. Berg would have stopped, but the torrent of his own thoughts carried him away. Night sank down upon them, the black forest night, where the scream of the owl shrills ghostly through the stillness. God came so near to them that the brightness of His throne dimmed the stars, and the angels of vengeance descended upon the mountain heights. And below them the flames of the underworld fluttered up to the outer curve of the earth and licked greedily at this last refuge of a race crushed by sin and woe.

.   .   .   .

Autumn came, and with it came storm. Tord went out alone into the woods to tend the traps and snares, while Berg remained at home to mend his clothes. The boy's path led him up a wooded height along which the falling leaves danced in circles in the gust. Again and again the feeling came to him that some one was walking behind him. He turned several times, then went on again when he had seen that it was only the wind and the leaves. He threatened the rustling circles with his fist, and kept on his way. But he had not silenced the sounds of his vision. At first it was the little dancing feet of elfin children; then it was the hissing of a great snake moving up behind him. Beside the snake there came a wolf, a tall, gray creature, waiting for the moment when the adder should strike at his feet to spring upon his back. Tord hastened his steps, but the visions hastened with him. When they seemed but two steps behind him, ready for the spring, he turned. There was nothing there, as he had known all the time. He sat down upon a stone to rest. The dried leaves played about his feet. The leaves of all the forest trees were there: the little yellow birch leaves, the red-tinged mountain ash leaves, the dried, black-brown foliage of the elm, the bright red aspen leaves, and the yellow-green fringes of the willows. Faded and crumpled, broken, and scarred, they were but little like the soft, tender shoots of green that had unrolled from the buds a few months ago.

"Ye are sinners," said the boy. "All of us are sinners. Nothing is pure in the eyes of God. Ye have already been shriveled up in the flame of His wrath."

Then he went on again, while the forest beneath him waved like a sea in storm, altho it was still and calm on the path around him. But he heard something he had never heard before. The wood was full of voices. Now it was like a whispering, now a gentle plaint, now a loud threat, or a roaring curse. It laughed, and it moaned. It was as the voice of hundreds. This unknown something that threatened and excited, that whistled and hissed, a something that seemed to be, and yet was not, almost drove him mad. He shivered in deadly terror, as he had shivered before, the day that he lay on the floor of his cave, and heard his pursuers rage over him through the forest. He seemed to hear again the crashing of the branches, the heavy footsteps of the men, the clanking of their arms, and their wild, bloodthirsty shouts.

It was not alone the storm that roared about him. There was something else in it, something yet more terrible; there were voices he could not understand, sounds as of a strange speech. He had heard many a mightier storm than this roar through the rigging. But he had never heard the wind playing on a harp of so many strings. Every tree seemed to have its own voice, every ravine had another song, the loud echo from the rocky wall shouted back in its own voice. He knew all these tones, but there were other stranger noises with them. And it was these that awoke a storm of voices within his own brain.

He had always been afraid when alone in the darkness of the wood. He loved the open sea and the naked cliffs. Ghosts and spirits lurked here in the shadows of the trees.

Then suddenly he knew who was speaking to him in the storm. It was God, the Great Avenger, the Lord of all Justice. God pursued him because of his comrade. God demanded that he should give up the murderer of the monk to vengeance.

Tord began to speak aloud amid the storm. He told God what he wanted to do, but that he could not do it. He had wanted to speak to the Giant and to beg him make his peace with God. But he could not find the words; embarrassment tied his tongue. "When I learned that the world is ruled by a God of Justice," he cried, "I knew that he was a lost man. I have wept through the night for my friend. I know that God will find him no matter where he may hide. But I could not speak to him; I could not find the words because of my love for him. Do not ask that I shall speak to him. Do not ask that the ocean shall rise to the height of the mountains."

He was silent again, and the deep voice of the storm, which he knew for God's voice, was silent also. There was a sudden pause in the wind, a burst of sunshine, a sound as of oars, and the gentle rustling of stiff reeds. These soft tones brought up the memory of Unn.

Then the storm began again, and he heard steps behind him, and a breathless panting. He did not dare to turn this time, for he knew that it was the white monk. He came from the banquet in Berg's great hall, covered with blood, and with an open ax cut in his forehead. And he whispered: "Betray him. Give him up, that you may save his soul."

Tord began to run. All this terror grew and grew in him, and he tried to flee from it. But as he ran he heard behind him the deep, mighty voice, which he knew was the voice of God. It was God himself pursuing him, demanding that he should give up the murderer. Berg's crime seemed more horrible to him than ever it had seemed before. A weaponless man had been murdered, a servant of God cut down by the steel. And the murderer still dared to live. He dared to enjoy the light of the sun and the fruits of the earth. Tord halted, clinched his fists, and shrieked a threat. Then, like a madman, he ran from the forest, the realm of terror, down into the valley.

．　　．　　．　　．　　．　　．　　．　　．

When Tord entered the cave the outlaw sat upon the bench of stone, sewing. The fire gave but a pale light, and the work did not seem to progress satisfactorily. The boy's heart swelled in pity. This superb Giant seemed all at once so poor and so unhappy.

"What is the matter?" asked Berg. "Are you ill? Have you been afraid?"

Then for the first time Tord spoke of his fear. "It was so strange in the forest. I heard the voices of spirits and I saw ghosts. I saw white monks."

"Boy!"

"They sang to me all the way up the slope to the hilltop. I ran from them, but they ran after me, singing. Can I not lay the spirits? What have I to do with them? There are others to whom their appearance is more necessary."

"Are you crazy to-night, Tord?"

Tord spoke without knowing what words he was using. His shyness had left him all at once, speech seemed to flow from his lips. "They were white monks, as pale as corpses. And their clothes are spotted with blood. They draw their hoods down over their foreheads, but I can see the wound shining there. The great, yawning, red wound from the ax."

"Tord," said the giant, pale and deeply grave, "the Saints alone know why you see wounds of ax thrusts. I slew the monk with a knife."

Tord stood before Berg trembling and wringing his hands. "They demand you of me. They would compel me to betray you."

"Who? The monks?"

"Yes, yes, the monks. They show me visions. They show me Unn. They show me the open, sunny ocean. They show me the camps of the fishermen, where there is dancing and merriment. I close my eyes, and yet I can see it all. 'Leave me,' I say to them. 'My friend has committed a murder, but he is not bad. Leave me alone, and I will talk to him, that he may repent and atone. He will see the wrong he has done, and he will make a pilgrimage to the Holy Grave.'"

"And what do the monks answer?" asked Berg. "They do not want to pardon me. They want to torture me and to burn me at the stake."

"'Shall I betray my best friend?' I ask them. He is all that I have in the world. He saved me from the bear when its claws were already at my throat. We have suffered hunger and cold together. He covered me with his own garments while I was ill. I have brought him wood and water, I have watched over his sleep and led his enemies off the trail. Why should they think me a man who betrays his friend? My friend will go to the priest himself, and will confess to him, and then together we will seek absolution."

Berg listened gravely, his keen eyes searching in Tord's face. "Go to the priest yourself, and tell him the truth. You must go back again among mankind."

"What does it help if I go alone? The spirits of the dead follow me because of your sin. Do you not see how I tremble before you? You have lifted your hand against God himself. What crime is like unto yours? Why did you tell me about the just God? It is you yourself who compel me to betray you. Spare me this sin. Go to the priest yourself." He sank down on his knees before Berg.

The murderer laid his hand on his head and looked at him. He measured his sin by the terror of his comrade, and it grew and grew to monstrous size. He saw himself in conflict with the Will that rules the world. Remorse entered his heart.

"Woe unto me that I did what I did," he said. "And is not this miserable life, this life we lead here in terror, and in deprivation, is it not atonement enough? Have I not lost home and fortune? Have I not lost friends, and all the joys that make the life of a man? What more?"

As he heard him speak thus, Tord sprang up in wild terror. "You can repent!" he cried. "My words move your heart? Oh, come with me, come at once. Come, let us go while there is yet time."

Berg the Giant sprang up also. "You—did it—?"

"Yes, yes, yes. I have betrayed you. But come quickly. Come now, now that you can repent. We must escape. We will escape."

The murderer stooped to the ground where the battle-ax of his fathers lay at his feet. "Son of a thief," he hissed. "I trusted you—I loved you."

But when Tord saw him stoop for the ax, he knew

that it was his own life that was in peril now. He tore
his own ax from his girdle, and thrust at Berg before
the latter could rise. The Giant fell headlong to the
floor, the blood spurting out over the cave. Between
the tangled masses of hair Tord saw the great, yawning,
red wound of an ax thrust.

Then the peasants stormed into the cave. They
praised his deed and told him that he should receive
full pardon.

Tord looked down at his hands, as if he saw there
the fetters that had drawn him on to kill the man he
loved. Like the chains of the Fenrir wolf, they were
woven out of empty air. They were woven out of the
green light amid the reeds, out of the play of shadows
in the woods, out of the song of the storm, out of the
rustling of the leaves, out of the magic vision of
dreams. And he said aloud: "God is great."

He crouched beside the body, spoke amid his tears
to the dead, and begged him to awake. The villagers
made a litter of their spears, on which to carry the
body of the free peasant to his home. The dead man
aroused awe in their souls, they softened their voices
in his presence. When they raised him to the bier,
Tord stood up, shook the hair from his eyes, and spoke
in a voice that trembled:

"Tell Unn, for whose sake Berg the Giant became
a murderer, that Tord the fisherman, whose father
plunders wrecks, and whose mother is a witch—tell her
that Tord slew Berg because Berg had taught him that
justice is the cornerstone of the world."

A CHANGE OF TREATMENT

By W. W. JACOBS

"Yes, I've sailed under some 'cute skippers in my time," said the night-watchman; "them that go down in big ships see the wonders o' the deep, you know," he added with a sudden chuckle, "but the one I'm going to tell you about ought never to have been trusted out without 'is ma. A good many o' my skippers had fads, but this one was the worst I ever sailed under.

"It's some few years ago now; I'd shipped on his bark, the John Elliott, as slow-going an old tub as ever I was aboard of, when I wasn't in quite a fit an' proper state to know what I was doing, an' I hadn't been in her two days afore I found out his 'obby through overhearing a few remarks made by the second mate, who came up from dinner in a hurry to make 'em. 'I don't mind saws an' knives hung round the cabin,' he ses to the fust mate, 'but when a chap has a 'uman 'and alongside 'is plate, studying it while folks is at their food, it's more than a Christian man can stand.'

" 'That's nothing,' ses the fust mate, who had sailed with the bark afore. 'He's half crazy on doctoring. We nearly had a mutiny aboard once owing to his wanting to hold a post mortem on a man what fell from the mast-head. Wanted to see what the poor feller died of.'

"'I call it unwholesome,' ses the second mate very savage. 'He offered me a pill at breakfast the size of a small marble; quite put me off my feed, it did.'

"Of course, the skipper's fad soon got known for'ard. But I didn't think much about it, till one day I seed old Dan'l Dennis sitting on a locker reading. Every now and then he'd shut the book, an' look up, closing 'is eyes, an' moving his lips like a hen drinking, an' then look down at the book again.

"'Why, Dan,' I ses, 'what's up? you ain't larning lessons at your time o' life?'

"'Yes, I am,' ses Dan very soft. 'You might hear me say it, it's this one about heart disease.'

"He hands over the book, which was stuck full o' all kinds o' diseases, and winks at me 'ard.

"'Picked it up on a book-stall,' he ses; then he shut 'is eyes an' said his piece wonderful. It made me quite queer to listen to 'im. 'That's how I feel,' ses he, when he'd finished. 'Just strength enough to get to bed. Lend a hand, Bill, an' go an' fetch the doctor.'

"Then I see his little game, but I wasn't going to run any risks, so I just mentioned, permiscous like, to the cook as old Dan seemed rather queer, an' went back an' tried to borrer the book, being always fond of reading. Old Dan pretended he was too ill to hear what I was saying, an' afore I could take it away from him, the skipper comes hurrying down with a bag in his 'and.

"'What's the matter, my man?' ses he, 'what's the matter?'

" 'I'm all right, sir,' ses old Dan, ' 'cept that I've been swoonding away a little.'

" 'Tell me exactly how you feel,' ses the skipper, feeling his pulse.

"Then old Dan said his piece over to him, an' the skipper shook his head an' looked very solemn.

" 'How long have you been like this?' he ses.

" 'Four or five years, sir,' ses Dan. 'It ain't nothing serious, sir, is it?'

" 'You lie quite still,' ses the skipper, putting a little trumpet thing to his chest an' then listening. 'Um! there's serious mischief here, I'm afraid; the prognotice is very bad.'

" 'Prog what, sir?' ses Dan, staring.

" 'Prognotice,' ses the skipper, at least I think that's the word he said. 'You keep perfectly still, an' I'll go an' mix you up a draft, an' tell the cook to get some strong beef-tea on."

"Well, the skipper 'ad no sooner gone, than Cornish Harry, a great big lumbering chap o' six feet two, goes up to old Dan, an' he ses, 'Gimme that book.'

" 'Go away,' says Dan, 'don't come worrying 'ere; you 'eard the skipper say how bad my prognotice was.'

" 'You lend me the book,' ses Harry, ketching hold of him, 'or else I'll bang you first, and split to the skipper arterward. I believe I'm a bit consumptive. Anyway, I'm going to see.'

"He dragged the book away from the old man, and began to study. There was so many complaints in it he was almost tempted to have something else instead of consumption, but he decided on that at last, an' he got a cough what worried the foc'sle all night long, an' the next day, when the skipper came down to see Dan, he could 'ardly 'ear hisself speak.

"'That's a nasty cough you've got, my man,' ses he, looking at Harry.

"'Oh, it's nothing, sir,' ses Harry, careless like. I've 'ad it for months now off and on. I think it's perspiring so of a night does it.'

"'What?' ses the skipper. 'Do you perspire of a night?'

"'Dredful,' ses Harry. 'You could wring the clo'es out. I s'pose it's healthy for me, ain't it, sir?'

"'Undo your shirt,' ses the skipper, going over to him, an' sticking the trumpet agin him. 'Now take a deep breath. Don't cough.'

"'I can't help it, sir,' ses Harry, 'it will come. Seems to tear me to pieces.'

"'You get to bed at once,' says the skipper, taking away the trumpet, an' shaking his 'ed. 'It's a fortunate thing for you, my lad, you're in skilled hands. With care, I believe I can pull you round. How does that medicine suit you, Dan?'

"'Beautiful, sir,' says Dan. 'It's wonderful soothing. I slep' like a new-born babe arter it.'

"'I'll send to get some more,' ses the skipper. 'You're not to get up, mind, either of you.'

"'All right, sir,' ses the two in very faint voices, an' the skipper went away arter telling us to be careful not to make a noise.

"We all thought it a fine joke at first, but the airs them two chaps give themselves was something sickening. Being in bed all day, they was naturally wakeful of a night, and they used to call across the foc'sle inquiring arter each other's healths, an' waking us other chaps up. An' they 'ud swop beef-tea an' jellies with each other, an' Dan 'ud try an coax a little port wine out o' Harry, which he 'ad to make blood with, but Harry 'ud say he hadn't made enough that day, an' he'd drink to the better health of old Dan's prognotice, an' smack his lips until it drove us a'most crazy to 'ear him.

"After these chaps had been ill two days, the other fellers began to put their heads together, being maddened by the smell o' beef-tea an' the like, an' said they was going to be ill too, and both the invalids got into a fearful state of excitement.

" 'You'll only spoil it for all of us,' ses Harry, 'and you don't know what to have without the book.'

" 'It's all very well doing your work as well as our own,' ses one of the men. 'It's our turn now. It's time you two got well.'

" 'Well?' ses Harry, 'well? Why, you silly iggernerant chaps, we shan't never get well; people with our complaints never do. You ought to know that.'

" 'Well, I shall split,' ses one of them.

" 'You do!' ses Harry, 'you do, an' I'll put a 'ed on you that all the port wine and jellies in the world wouldn't cure. 'Sides, don't you think the skipper knows what's the matter with us?'

" 'Afore the other chaps could reply, the skipper hisself comes down, accompanied by the fust mate with a look on his face which made Harry give th deepest and hollowest cough he'd ever done.

" 'What they reely want,' ses the skipper, turnin; to the mate, 'is keerful nussing.'

" 'I wish you'd let me nuss 'em,' ses the fust mate 'only ten minutes—I'd put 'em both on their legs an' running for their lives into the bargain, in ten minutes.'

" 'Hold your tongue, sir,' ses the skipper; 'wha

you say is unfeeling, besides being an insult to me. Do you think I studied medicine all these years without knowing when a man's ill?'

"The fust mate growled something, and went on deck and the skipper started examining of 'em again. He said they was wonderfully patient lying in bed so long, an' he had 'em wrapped up in bed clo'es and carried on deck, so as the pure air could have a go at 'em.

"We had to do the carrying, an' there they sat, breathing the pure air, and looking at the fust mate out of the corners of their eyes. If they wanted any thing from below, one of us had to go an' fetch it, an' by the time they was taken down to bed again, we all resolved to be took ill too.

"Only two of 'em did it tho, for Harry, who was a powerful, ugly-tempered chap, swore he'd do all sorts o' dreadful things to us if we didn't keep well and hearty, an' all 'cept these two did. One of 'em, Mike Rafferty, laid up with a swelling on his ribs, which I knew myself he 'ad 'ad for fifteen years, and the other chap had paralysis. I never saw a man so reely happy as the skipper was. He was up an' down with his medicines and his instruments all day long, and used to make notes of the cases in a big pocketbook, and read 'em to the second mate at meal-times.

"The foc'sle had been turned into hospital about a week, an' I was on deck doing some odd job or the other, when the cook comes up to me pulling a face as long as a fiddle.

" ' 'Nother invalid,' ses he; 'fust mate's gone stark, staring mad!'

" 'Mad?' ses I.

" 'Yes,' ses he. 'He's got a big basin in the galley,

S. S. VIII-4

an' he's laughing like a hyener an' mixing bilge-water an' ink, an' paraffin an' butter an' soap an' all sorts o' things up together. The smell's enough to kill a man; I've had to come away.'

"Curious-like, I jest walked up to the galley an' puts my 'ed in, an' there was the mate as the cook said, smiling all over his face, and ladling some thick sticky stuff into a stone bottle.

"How's the pore sufferers, sir?' ses he, stepping out of the galley jest as the skipper was going by.

" 'They're very bad; but I hope for the best,' ses the skipper, looking at him hard. 'I'm glad to see you're turned a bit more feeling.'

" 'Yes,' ses the mate. 'I didn't think so at fust, but I can see now them chaps is all very ill. You'll s'cuse me saying it, but I don't quite approve of your treatment.'

"I thought the skipper would ha' bust.

" 'My treatment?' ses he. 'My treatment? What do you know about it?'

" 'You're treating 'em wrong, sir,' ses the mate. 'I have here' (patting the jar) 'a remedy which 'ud cure them all if you'd only let me try it.'

" 'Pooh!' ses the skipper. 'One medicine cure all diseases! The old story. What is it? Where'd you get it from?' ses he.

" 'I brought the ingredients aboard with me,' ses the mate. 'It's a wonderful medicine discovered by my grandmother, an' if I might only try it I'd thoroughly cure them pore chaps.'

" 'Rubbish!' ses the skipper.

" 'Very well, sir,' ses the mate, shrugging his shoulders. 'O' course, if you won't let me you won't. Still,

I tell you, if you'd let me try I'd cure 'em all in two days. That's a fair challenge.'

"Well, they talked, and talked, and talked, until at last the skipper give way and went down below with the mate, and told the chaps they was to take the new medicine for two days, jest to prove the mate was wrong.

" 'Let pore old Dan try it first, sir,' ses Harry, starting up, an' sniffing as the mate took the cork out; 'he's been awful bad since you've been away.'

" 'Harry's worse than I am, sir,' ses Dan, 'it's only his kind heart that makes him say that.'

" 'It don't matter which is fust,' ses the mate, filling a tablespoon with it, 'there's plenty for all. Now, Harry.'

" 'Take it,' ses the skipper.

"Harry took it, an' the fuss he made you'd ha' thought he was swallering a football. It stuck all round his mouth, and he carried on so dredful that the other invalids was half sick afore it came to them.

"By the time the other three 'ad 'ad theirs it was as good as a pantermine, an' the mate corked the bottle up, and went an' sat down on a locker while they tried to rinse their mouths out with the luxuries which had been given 'em.

" 'How do you feel?' ses the skipper.

" 'I'm dying,' ses Dan.

" 'So'm I,' ses Harry; 'I b'leeve the mate's pisoned us.'

"The skipper looks over the mate very stern an' shakes his 'ed slowly.

" 'It's all right,' ses the mate. 'It's always like that the first dozen or so doses.'

" 'Dozen or so doses!' ses old Dan, in a faraway voice.

" 'It has to be taken every twenty minutes,' ses the mate, pulling out his pipe and lighting it; an' the four men groaned all together.

" 'I can't allow it,' ses the skipper, 'I can't allow it. Men's lives mustn't be sacrificed for an experiment.'

" ' 'Tain't a experiment,' ses the mate very indignant, 'it's an old family medicine.'

" 'Well, they shan't have any more,' ses the skipper firmly.

" 'Look here,' ses the mate. 'If I kill any one o' these men, I'll give you twenty pound. Honor bright, I will.'

" 'Make it twenty-five,' ses the skipper, considering.

" 'Very good,' ses the mate. 'Twenty-five; I can't say no fairer than that, can I? It's about time for another dose now.'

"He gave 'em another tablespoonful all round as the skipper left, an't the chaps what wasn't invalids nearly bust with joy. He wouldn't let 'em have anything to take the taste out, 'cos he said it didn't give the medicine a chance, an' he told us other chaps to remove the temptation, an' you bet we did.

"After the fifth dose, the invalids began to get desperate, an' when they heard they'd got to be woke up every twenty minutes through the night to take the stuff, they sort o' give up. Old Dan said he felt a gentle glow stealing over him and strengthening him, and Harry said that it felt like a healing balm to his lungs. All of 'em agreed it was a wonderful sort o' medicine, an' arter the sixth dose the man with paralysis dashed upon deck, and ran up the rigging like a cat. He sat there for hours spitting, an' swore he'd brain anybody who interrupted him, an' arter a little while Mike Rafferty went up and j'ined him, an' if the fust mate's ears didn't burn by reason of the things them two pore sufferers said about 'im, they ought to.

"They was all doing full work next day, an' tho, o' course, the skipper saw how he'd been done, he didn't allude to it. Not in words, that is; but when a man tries to make four chaps do the work of eight, an' hits 'em when they don't, it's a easy job to see where the shoe pinches."

THE THIEF

By Feodor Mikailovitch Dostoievski

One morning, just as I was about to leave for my place of employment, Agrafena (my cook, laundress, and housekeeper all in one person) entered my room, and, to my great astonishment, started a conversation.

She was a quiet, simple-minded woman, who during the whole six years of her stay with me had never spoken more than two or three words daily, and that in reference to my dinner—at least, I had never heard her.

"I have come to you, sir," she suddenly began, "about the renting out of the little spare room."

"What spare room?"

"The one that is near the kitchen, of course; which should it be?"

"Why?"

"Why do people generally take lodgers? Because."

"But who will take it?"

"Who will take it! A lodger, of course! Who should take it?"

"But there is hardly room in there, mother mine, for a bed; it will be too cramped. How can one live in it?"

"But why live in it! He only wants a place to sleep in; he will live on the window-seat."

"What window-seat?"

"How is that? What window-seat? As if you did not know! The one in the hall. He will sit on it and sew, or do something else. But maybe he will sit on a chair; he has a chair of his own—and a table also, and everything."

"But who is he?"

"A nice, worldly-wise man. I will cook for him and will charge him only three rubles in silver a month for room and board—"

At last, after long endeavor, I found out that some elderly man had talked Agrafena into taking him into the kitchen as lodger. When Agrafena once got a thing into her head that thing had to be done; otherwise I knew I would have no peace. On those occasions when things did go against her wishes, she immediately fell into a sort of brooding, became exceedingly melancholy, and continued in that state for two or three weeks. During this time the food was invariably spoiled, the linen was missing, the floors unscrubbed; in a word, a lot of unpleasant things happened. I had long ago become aware of the fact that this woman of very few words was incapable of forming a decision or of coming to any conclusion based on her own thoughts; and yet when it happened that by some means there had formed in her weak brain a sort of idea or wish to undertake a thing, to refuse her permission to carry out this idea or wish meant simply to kill her morally for some time. And so, acting in the sole interest of my peace of mind, I immediately agreed to this new proposition of hers.

"Has he at least the necessary papers, a passport, or anything of the kind?"

"How then? Of course he has. A fine man like

him—who has seen the world— He promised to pay three rubles a month."

On the very next day the new lodger appeared in my modest bachelor quarters; but I did not feel annoyed in the least—on the contrary, in a way I was glad of it. I live a very solitary, hermit-like life. I have almost no acquaintance and seldom go out. Having led the existence of a moor-cock for ten years, I was naturally used to solitude. But ten, fifteen years or more of the same seclusion in company with a person like Agrafena, and in the same bachelor dwelling, was indeed a joyless prospect. Therefore, the presence of another quiet, unobtrusive man in the house was, under these circumstances, a real blessing.

Agrafena had spoken the truth: the lodger was a man who had seen much in his life. From his passport it appeared that he was a retired soldier, which I noticed even before I looked at the passport.

As soon as I glanced at him in fact.

Astafi Ivanich, my lodger, belonged to the better sort of soldiers, another thing I noticed as soon as I saw him. We liked each other from the first, and our life flowed on peacefully and comfortably. The best thing was that Astafi Ivanich could at times tell a good story, incidents of his own life. In the general tediousness of my humdrum existence, such a narrator was a veritable treasure. Once he told me a story which has made a lasting impression upon me; but first the incident which led to the story.

Once I happened to be left alone in the house, Astafi and Agrafena having gone out on business. Suddenly I heard some one enter, and I felt that it must be a stranger; I went out into the corridor and

found a man of short stature and notwithstanding the
cold weather, dressed very thinly and without an
overcoat.

"What is it you want?"

"The Government clerk Alexandrov? Does he live
here?"

"There is no one here by that name, little brother;
good day."

"The porter told me he lived here," said the visitor,
cautiously retreating toward the door.

"Go on, go on, little brother; be off!"

Soon after dinner the next day, when Astafi brought
in my coat, which he had repaired for me, I once
more heard a strange step in the corridor. I opened
the door.

The visitor of the day before, calmly and before my
very eyes, took my short coat from the rack, put it
under his arm, and ran out.

Agrafena, who had all the time been looking at
him in open-mouthed surprize through the kitchen
door, seemingly unable to stir from her place and
rescue the coat. But Astafi Ivanich rushed after the
rascal, and, out of breath and panting, returned empty-
handed. The man had vanished as if the earth had
swallowed him.

"It is too bad, really, Astafi Ivanich," I said. "It
is well that I have my cloak left. Otherwise the scoun-
drel would have put me out of service altogether."

But Astafi seemed so much affected by what had
happened that as I gazed at him I forgot all about
the theft. He could not regain his composure, and
every once in a while threw down the work which
occupied him, and began once more to recount how it
had all happened, where he had been standing, while

only two steps away my coat had been stolen before his very eyes, and how he could not even catch the thief. Then once more he resumed his work, only to throw it away again, and I saw him go down to the porter, tell him what had happened, and reproach him with not taking sufficient care of the house, that such a theft could be perpetrated in it. When he returned he began to upbraid Agrafena. Then he again resumed his work, muttering to himself for a long time—how this is the way it all was—how he stood here, and I there, and how before our very eyes, no farther than two steps away, the coat was taken off its hanger, and so on. In a word, Astafi Ivanich, tho he knew how to do certain things, worried a great deal over trifles.

"We have been fooled, Astafi Ivanich," I said to him that evening, handing him a glass of tea, and hoping from sheer ennui to call forth the story of the lost coat again, which by dint of much repetition had begun to sound extremely comical.

"Yes, we were fooled, sir. It angers me very much, tho the loss is not mine, and I think there is nothing so despicably low in this world as a thief. They steal what you buy by working in the sweat of your brow— Your time and labor— The loathsome creature! It sickens me to talk of it—pfui! It makes me angry to think of it. How is it, sir, that you do not seem to be at all sorry about it?"

"To be sure, Astafi Ivanich, one would much sooner see his things burn up than see a thief take them. It is exasperating—"

"Yes, it is annoying to have anything stolen from you. But of course there are thieves and thieves—I, for instance, met an honest thief through an accident."

"How is that? An honest thief? How can a thief be honest, Astafi Ivanich?"

"You speak truth, sir. A thief can not be an honest man. There never was such. I only wanted to say that he was an honest man, it seems to me, even tho he stole. I was very sorry for him."

"And how did it happen, Astafi Ivanich?"

"It happened just two years ago. I was serving as house steward at the time, and the baron whom I served expected shortly to leave for his estate, so that I knew I would soon be out of a job, and then God only knew how I would be able to get along; and just then it was that I happened to meet in a tavern a poor forlorn creature, Emelian by name. Once upon a time he had served somewhere or other, but had been driven out of service on account of tippling. Such an unworthy creature as he was! He wore whatever came along. At times I even wondered if he wore a shirt under his shabby cloak; everything he could put his hands on was sold for drink. But he was not a rowdy. Oh, no; he was of a sweet, gentle nature, very kind and tender to every one; he never asked for anything, was, if anything, too conscientious— Well, you could see without asking when the poor fellow was dying for a drink, and of course you treated him to one. Well, we became friendly, that is, he attached himself to me like a little dog—you go this way, he follows—and all this after our very first meeting.

"Of course he remained with me that night; his passport was in order and the man seemed all right. On the second night also. On the third he did not leave the house, sitting on the window-seat of the corridor the whole day, and of course he remained over that night too. Well, I thought, just see how he has forced himself upon you. You have to give him to eat and to drink and to shelter him. All a poor man needs is some one to sponge upon him. I soon found out that once before he had attached himself to a man just as he had now attached himself to me; they drank together, but the other one soon died of some deep-seated sorrow. I thought and thought: What shall I do with him? Drive him out—my conscience would not allow it—I felt very sorry for him: he was such a wretched, forlorn creature, terrible! And so dumb he did not ask for anything, only sat quietly and looked you straight in the eyes, just like a faithful little dog. That is how drink can ruin a man. And I thought to myself: Well, suppose I say to him: 'Get out of here, Emelian; you have nothing to do in here, you come to the wrong person; I will soon have nothing to eat myself, so how do you expect me to feed *you?*' And I tried to imagine what he would do after I'd told him all this. And I could see how he would look at me for a long time after he had heard me, without understanding a word; how at last he would understand what I was driving at, and, rising from the window-seat, take his little bundle —I see it before me now—a red-checked little bundle full of holes, in which he kept God knows what, and which he carted along with him wherever he went; how he would brush and fix up his worn cloak a little, so that it would look a bit more decent and not show so much the holes and patches—he was a man of very fine feelings! How he would have opened the door afterward and would have gone forth with tears in his eyes.

"Well, should a man be allowed to perish altogether?

I all at once felt heartily sorry for him; but at the
same time I thought: And what about me, am I
any better off? And I said to myself: Well, Emelian,
you will not feast overlong at my expense; soon I
shall have to move from here myself, and then you
will not find me again. Well, sir, my baron soon left
for his estate with all his household, telling me before
he went that he was very well satisfied with my services, and would gladly employ me again on his return
to the capital. A fine man my baron was, but he died
the same year.

"Well, after I had escorted my baron and his family
a little way, I took my things and the little money I
had saved up, and went to live with an old woman
I knew, who rented out a corner of the room she
occupied by herself. She used to be a nurse in some
well-to-do family, and now, in her old age, they had
pensioned her off. Well, I thought to myself, now
it is good-by to you, Emelian, dear man, you will not
find me now! And what do you think, sir? When
I returned in the evening—I had paid a visit to an
acquaintance of mine—whom should I see but Emelian
sitting quietly upon my trunk with his red-checked
bundle by his side. He was wrapped up in his poor
little cloak, and was awaiting my home-coming. He
must have been quite lonesome, because he had borrowed a prayer-book of the old woman and held it
upside down. He had found me after all! My hands
fell helplessly at my sides. Well, I thought, there is
nothing to be done, why did I not drive him away first
off? And I only asked him: 'Have you taken your
passport along, Emelian?' Then I sat down, sir, and
began to turn the matter over in my mind: Well, could
e, a roving man, be much in my way? And after

I had considered it well, I decided that he would not,
and besides, he would be of very little expense to me.
Of course, he would have to be fed, but what does that
amount to? Some bread in the morning and, to make
it a little more appetizing, a little onion or so. For
the midday meal again some bread and onion, and
for the evening again onion and bread, and some kvass,
and, if some cabbage-soup should happen to come
our way, then we could both fill up to the throat.
I ate little, and Emelian, who was a drinking man,
surely ate almost nothing: all he wanted was vodka.
He would be the undoing of me with his drinking; but
at the same time I felt a curious feeling creep over
me. It seemed a if life would be a burden to me if
Emelian went away. And so I decided then and there
to be his father-benefactor. I would put him on his
legs, I thought, save him from perishing, and gradually
wean him from drink. Just you wait, I thought. Stay
with me, Emelian, but stand pat now. Obey the word
of command!

"Well, I thought to myself, I will begin by teaching
him some work, but not at once; let him first enjoy
himself a bit, and I will in the mean while look around
and discover what he finds easiest, and would be
capable of doing, because you must know, sir, a man
must have a calling and a capacity for a certain work
to be able to do it properly. And I began stealthily
to observe him. And a hard subject he was, that
Emelian! At first I tried to get at him with a kind
word. Thus and thus I would speak to him: 'Emelian
you had better take more care of yourself and try to
fix yourself up a little.

"'Give up drinking. Just look at yourself, man
you are all ragged, your cloak looks more like a sieve

than anything else. It is not nice. It is about time
for you to come to your senses and know when you
have had enough.'

"He listened to me, my Emelian did, with lowered
head; he had already reached that state, poor fellow,
when the drink affected his tongue and he could not
utter a sensible word. You talk to him about cucum-
bers, and he answers beans. He listened, listened to
me for a long time, and then he would sigh deeply.

" 'What are you sighing for, Emelian?' I ask him.

" 'Oh, it is nothing, Astafi Ivanich, do not worry.
Only what I saw to-day, Astafi Ivanich—two women
fighting about a basket of huckleberries that one of
them had upset by accident.'

" 'Well, what of that?'

" 'And the woman whose berries were scattered
snatched a like basket of huckleberries from the other
woman's hand, and not only threw them on the ground,
but stamped all over them.'

" 'Well, but what of that, Emelian?'

" 'Ech!' I think to myself, 'Emelian! You have
lost your poor wits through the cursed drink!'

" 'And again,' Emelian says, 'a baron lost a bill on
the Gorokhova Street—or was it on the Sadova? A
muzhik saw him drop it, and says, "My luck," but
here another one interfered and says, "No, it is my
luck! I saw it first. . . ." '

" 'Well, Emelian?'

" 'And the two muzhiks started a fight, Astafi
Ivanich, and the upshot was that a policeman came,
picked up the money, handed it back to the baron,
and threatened to put the muzhiks under lock for
raising a disturbance.'

" 'But what of that? What is there wonderful or edifying in that, Emelian?'

" 'Well, nothing, but the people laughed, Astafi Ivanich.'

" 'E-ch, Emelian! What have the people to do with it?' I said. 'You have sold your immortal soul for a copper. But do you know what I will tell you, Emelian?'

" 'What, Astafi Ivanich?'

" 'You'd better take up some work, really you should. I am telling you for the hundredth time that you should have pity on yourself!'

" 'But what shall I do, Astafi Ivanich? I do not know where to begin and no one would employ me, Astafi Ivanich.'

" 'That is why they drove you out of service, Emelian; it is all on account of drink!'

" 'And to-day,' said Emelian, 'they called Vlass the barkeeper into the office.'

" 'What did they call him for, Emelian?' I asked.

" 'I don't know why, Astafi Ivanich. I suppose it was needed, so they called him.'

" 'Ech,' I thought to myself, 'no good will come of either of us, Emelian! It is for our sins that God is punishing us!'

"Well, what could a body do with such a man, sir!

"But he was sly, the fellow was, I tell you! He listened to me, listened, and at last it seems it began to tire him, and as quick as he would notice that I was growing angry he would take his cloak and slip out—and that was the last to be seen of him! He would not show up the whole day, and only in the evening would he return, as drunk as a lord. Who treated him to drinks, or where he got the money for it, God only knows; not from me, surely!   . . .

" 'Well,' I say to him, 'Emelian, you will have to give up drink, do you hear? you will have to give it up! The next time you return tipsy, you will have to sleep on the stair. I'll not let you in!'

"After this Emelian kept to the house for two days; on the third he once more sneaked out. I wait and wait for him; he does not come! I must confess that I was kind of frightened; besides, I felt terribly sorry for him. What had I done to the poor devil; I thought. I must have frightened him off. Where could he have gone to now, the wretched creature? Great God, he may perish yet! The night passed and he did not return. In the morning I went out into the hall, and he was lying there with his head on the lower step, almost stiff with cold.

" 'What is the matter with you, Emelian? The Lord save you! Why are you here?'

" 'But you know, Astafi Ivanich,' he replied, 'you were angry with me the other day; I aggravated you, and you promised to make me sleep in the hall, and I—so I—did not dare—to come in—and lay down here.'

" 'It would be better for you, Emelian,' I said, filled with anger and pity, 'to find a better employment than needlessly watching the stairs!'

" 'But what other employment, Astafi Ivanich?'

" 'Well, wretched creature that you are,' here anger had flamed up in me, "if you would try to learn the tailoring art. Just look at the cloak you are wearing! Not only is it full of holes, but you are sweeping the stairs with it! You should at least take a needle and mend it a little, so it would look more decent. E-ch, a wretched tippler you are, and nothing more!'

"Well, sir! What do you think! He did take the needle—I had told him only for fun, and there he got scared and actually took the needle. He threw off his cloak and began to put the thread through; well, it was easy to see what would come of it; his eyes began to fill and reddened, his hands trembled! He pushed and pushed the thread—could not get it through: he wetted it, rolled it between his fingers, smoothed it out, but it would not—go! He flung it from him and looked at me.

" 'Well, Emelian!' I said, 'you served me right! If people had seen it I would have died with shame! I only told you all this for fun, and because I was angry with you. Never mind sewing; may the Lord keep you from sin! You need not do anything, only keep out of mischief, and do not sleep on the stairs and put me to shame thereby!'

" 'But what shall I do, Astafi Ivanich; I know myself that I am always tipsy and unfit for anything! I only make you, my be—benefactor, angry for nothing.'

"And suddenly his bluish lips began to tremble, and a tear rolled down his unshaven, pale cheek, then another and another one, and he broke into a very flood of tears, my Emelian. Father in Heaven! I felt as if some one had cut me over the heart with a knife.

" 'E-ch you, sensitive man; why, I never thought And who *could* have thought such a thing! No, I'd better give you up altogether, Emelian; do as you please.'

"Well, sir, what else is there to tell! But the whole thing is so insignificant and unimportant, it is really not worth while wasting words about it; for instance you, sir, would not give two broken groschen for it but I, I would give much, if I had much, that this thing had never happened! I owned, sir, a pair of breeches, blue, in checks, a first-class article, the devil take them—a rich landowner who came here on business ordered them from me, but refused afterward to take them, saying that they were too tight, and left them with me.

"Well, I thought, the cloth is of first-rate quality! I can get five rubles for them in the old-clothes market-place, and, if not, I can cut a fine pair of pantaloons out of them for some St. Petersburg gent, and have a piece left over for a vest for myself. Everything counts with a poor man! And Emelian was at that time in sore straits. I saw that he had given up drinking, first one day, then a second, and a third, and looked so downhearted and sad.

"Well, I thought, it is either that the poor fellow lacks the necessary coin or maybe he has entered on the right path, and has at last listened to good sense.

"Well, to make a long story short, an important holiday came just at that time, and I went to vespers. When I came back I saw Emelian sitting on the window-seat as drunk as a lord. Eh! I thought, so that is what you are about! And I go to my trunk to get out something I needed. I look! The breeches are not there. I rummage about in this place and that place: gone! Well, after I had searched all over and saw that they were missing for fair, I felt as if something had gone through me! I went after the old woman—as to Emelian, tho there was evidence against him in his being drunk, I somehow never thought of him!

" 'No,' says my old woman; 'the good Lord keep you, gentleman, what do I need breeches for? can I wear them? I myself missed a skirt the other day. I know nothing at all about it.'

"'Well,' I asked, 'has any one called here?'

"'No one called,' she said. 'I was in all the time; your friend here went out for a short while and then came back; here he sits! Why don't you ask him?'

"'Did you happen, for some reason or other, Emelian, to take the breeches out of the trunk? The ones, you remember, which were made for the landowner?'

"'No,' he says, 'I have not taken them, Astafi Ivanich.'

"'What *could* have happened to them?' Again I began to search, but nothing came of it! And Emelian sat and swayed to and fro on the windowseat.

"I was on my knees before the open trunk, just in front of him. Suddenly I threw a side-long glance at him. Ech, I thought, and felt very hot round the heart, and my face grew very red. Suddenly my eyes encountered Emelian's.

"'No,' he says, 'Astafi Ivanich. You perhaps think that I—you know what I mean—but I have not taken them.'

"'But where have they gone, Emelian?'

"'No,' he says, 'Astafi Ivanich, I have not seen them at all.'

"'Well, then, you think they simply went and got lost by themselves, Emelian?'

"'Maybe they did, Astafi Ivanich.'

"After this I would not waste another word on him. I rose from my knees, locked the trunk, and after I had lighted the lamp I sat down to work. I was remaking a vest for a government clerk, who lived on the floor below. But I was terribly rattled, just the same. It would have been much easier to bear, I thought, if all my wardrobe had burned to ashes. Emelian, it seems, felt that I was deeply angered. It is always so, sir, when a man is guilty; he always feels beforehand when trouble approaches, as a bird feels the coming storm.

"'And do you know, Astafi Ivanich,' he suddenly began, 'the leach married the coachman's widow to-day.'

"I just looked at him; but, it seems, looked at him so angrily that he understood: I saw him rise from his seat, approach the bed, and begin to rummage in it, continually repeating: 'Where could they have gone, vanished, as if the devil had taken them!'

"I waited to see what was coming; I saw that my Emelian had crawled under the bed. I could contain myself no longer.

"'Look here,' I said. 'What makes you crawl under the bed?'

"'I am looking for the breeches, Astafi Ivanich,' said Emelian from under the bed. 'Maybe they got here somehow or other.'

"'But what makes you, sir (in my anger I addressed him as if he was—somebody), what makes you trouble yourself on account of such a plain man as I am; dirtying your knees for nothing!'

"'But, Astafi Ivanich— I did not mean anything— I only thought maybe if we look for them here we may find them yet.'

"'Mm! Just listen to me a moment, Emelian!'

"'What, Astafi Ivanich?'

"'Have you not simply stolen them from me like a rascally thief, serving me so for my bread and salt?'

I said to him, beside myself with wrath at the sight of him crawling under the bed for something he knew was not there.

" 'No, Astafi Ivanich.' For a long time he remained lying flat under the bed. Suddenly he crawled out and stood before me—I seem to see him even now—as terrible a sight as sin itself.

" 'No,' he says to me in a trembling voice, shivering through all his body and pointing to his breast with his finger, so that all at once I became scared and could not move from my seat on the window. 'I have not taken your breeches, Astafi Ivanich.'

" 'Well,' I answered, 'Emelian, forgive me if in my foolishness I have accused you wrongfully. As to the breeches, let them go hang; we will get along without them. We have our hands, thank God, we will not have to steal, and now, too, we will not have to sponge on another poor man; we will earn our living.'

"Emelian listened to me and remained standing before me for some time, then he sat down and sat motionless the whole evening; when I lay down to sleep he was still sitting in the same place.

"In the morning, when I awoke, I found him sleeping on the bare floor, wrapped up in his cloak; he felt his humiliation so strongly that he had no heart to go and lie down on the bed.

"Well, sir, from that day on I conceived a terrible dislike for the man; that is, rather I hated him the first few days, feeling as if, for instance, my own son had robbed me and given me deadly offense. Ech, I thought, Emelian, Emelian! And Emelian, my dear sir, had gone on a two weeks' spree. Drunk to bestiality from morning till night. And during the whole two weeks he had not uttered a word. I suppose he was consumed the whole time by a deep-seated grief, or else he was trying in this way to make an end to himself. At last he gave up drinking. I suppose he had no longer the wherewithal to buy vodka—had drunk up every copeck—and he once more took up his old place on the window-seat. I remember that he sat there for three whole days without a word; suddenly I see him weep; sit there and cries, but what crying! The tears come from his eyes in showers, drip, drip, as if he did not know that he was shedding them. It is very painful, sir, to see a grown man weep, all the more when the man is of advanced years, like Emelian, and cries from grief and a sorrowful heart.

"'What ails you, Emelian?' I say to him.

"He starts and shivers. This was the first time I had spoken to him since that eventful day.

"It is nothing—Astafi Ivanich.'

"'God keep you, Emelian; never you mind it all. Let bygones be bygones. Don't take it to heart so, man!' I felt very sorry for him.

"'It is only that—that I would like to do something—some kind of work, Astafi Ivanich.'

"'But what kind of work, Emelian?'

"'Oh, any kind. Maybe I will go into some kind of service, as before. I have already been at my former employer's asking. It will not do for me, Astafi Ivanich, to use you any longer. I, Astafi Ivanich, will perhaps obtain some employment, and then I will pay you for everything, food and all.'

"'Don't, Emelian, don't. Well, let us say you committed a sin; well, it is over! The devil take it all! Let us live as before—as if nothing had happened!'"

" 'You, Astafi Ivanich, you are probably hinting about *that*. But I have not taken your breeches.'

" 'Well, just as you please, Emelian!'

" 'No, Astafi Ivanich, evidently I can not live with you longer. You will excuse me, Astafi Ivanich.'

" 'But God be with you, Emelian,' I said to him; 'who is it that is offending you or driving you out of the house? Is it I who am doing it?'

" 'No, but it is unseemly for me to misuse your hospitality any longer, Astafi Ivanich; 'twill be better to go.'

"I saw that he had in truth risen from his place and donned his ragged cloak—he felt offended, the man did, and had gotten it into his head to leave, and—basta.

" 'But where are you going, Emelian? Listen to sense: what are you? Where will you go?'

" 'No, it is best so, Astafi Ivanich, do not try to keep me back,' and he once more broke into tears; 'let me be, Astafi Ivanich, you are no longer what you used to be.'

" 'Why am I not? I am just the same. But you will perish when left alone—like a foolish little child, Emelian.'

" 'No, Astafi Ivanich. Lately, before you leave the house, you have taken to locking your trunk, and I, Astafi Ivanich, see it and weep—No, it is better you should let me go, Astafi Ivanich, and forgive me if I have offended you in any way during the time we have lived together.'

"Well, sir! And so he did go away. I waited a day and thought: Oh, he will be back toward evening. But a day passes, then another, and he does not return. On the third—he does not return. I grew frightened, and a terrible sadness gripped at my heart. I stopped eating and drinking, and lay whole nights without closing my eyes. The man had wholly disarmed me! On the fourth day I went to look for him; I looked in all the taverns and pot-houses in the vicinity, and asked if any one had seen him. No, Emelian had wholly disappeared! Maybe he has done away with his miserable existence, I thought. Maybe, when in his cups, he has perished like a dog, somewhere under a fence. I came home half dead with fatigue and despair, and decided to go out the next day again to look for him, cursing myself bitterly for the letting the foolish, helpless man go away from me. But at dawn of the fifth day (it was a holiday) I heard the door creak. And whom should I see but Emelian! But in what a state! His face was bluish and his hair was full of mud, as if he had slept in the street; and he had grown thin, the poor fellow had as thin as a rail. He took off his poor cloak, sat down on my trunk, and began to look at me. Well, sir, I was overjoyed, but at the same time felt a greater sadness than ever pulling at my heart-strings. This is how it was, sir: I felt that if a thing like that had happened to me, that is—I would sooner have perished like a dog, but would not have returned. And Emelian did. Well, naturally, it is hard to see a man in such a state. I began to coddle and to comfort him in every way.

"'Well,' I said, 'Emelian, I am very glad you have returned; if you had not come so soon, you would not have found me in, as I intended to go hunting for you. Have you had anything to eat?'

"'I have eaten, Astafi Ivanich.'

"'I doubt it. Well, here is some cabbage soup—

left over from yesterday; a nice soup with some meat in it—not the meager kind. And here you have some bread and a little onion. Go ahead and eat; it will do you good.'

"I served it to him; and immediately realized that he must have been starving for the last three days— such an appetite as he showed! So it was hunger that had driven him back to me. Looking at the poor fellow, I was deeply touched, and decided to run into the nearby dram-shop. I will get him some vodka, I thought, to liven him up a bit and make peace with him. It is enough. I have nothing against the poor devil any longer. And so I brought the vodka and said to him: 'Here, Emelian, let us drink to each other's health in honor of the holiday. Come, take a drink. It will do you good.'

"He stretched out his hand, greedily stretched it out, you know, and stopped; then, after a while, he lifted the glass, carried it to his mouth, spilling the liquor on his sleeve; at last he did carry it to his mouth, but immediately put it back on the table.

" 'Well, why don't you drink, Emelian?'

" 'But no, I'll not, Astafi Ivanich.'

" 'You'll not drink it!'

" 'But I, Astafi Ivanich, I think—I'll not drink any more, Astafi Ivanich.'

" 'Is it for good you have decided to give it up, Emelian, or only for to-day?'

"He did not reply, and after a while I saw him lean his head on his hand, and I asked him: 'Are you not feeling well, Emelian?'

" 'Yes, pretty well, Astafi Ivanich.'

"I made him go to bed, and saw that he was truly in a bad way. His head was burning hot and he was shivering with ague. I sat by him the whole day; toward evening he grew worse. I prepared a meal for him of kvass, butter, and some onion, and threw in it a few bits of bread, and said to him: 'Go ahead and take some food; maybe you will feel better!'

"But he only shook his head: 'No, Astafi Ivanich, I shall not have any dinner to-day.'

"I had some tea prepared for him, giving a lot of trouble to the poor old woman from whom I rented a part of the room—but he would not take even a little tea.

"Well, I thought to myself, it is a bad case. On the third morning, I went to see the doctor, an acquaintance of mine, Dr. Kostopravov, who had treated me when I still lived in my last place. The doctor came, examined the poor fellow, and only said: 'There was no need of sending for me, he is already too far gone, but you can give him some powders which I will prescribe.'

"Well, I didn't give him the powders at all, as I understood that the doctor was only doing it for form's sake; and in the meanwhile came the fifth day.

"He lay dying before me, sir. I sat on the window-seat with some work I had on hand lying on my lap. The old woman was raking the stove. We were all silent, and my heart was breaking over this poor, shiftless creature, as if he were my own son whom I was losing. I knew that Emelian was gazing at me all the time; I noticed for the earliest morning that he longed to tell me something, but seemingly dared not. At last I looked at him, and saw that he did not take his eyes from me, but that whenever his eyes met mine, he immediately lowered his own.

" 'Astafi Ivanich!'

" 'What, Emelian?'

" 'What if my cloak should be carried over to the old clothes market, would they give much for it, Astafi Ivanich?'

" 'Well,' I said, 'I do not know for certain, but three rubles they would probably give for it, Emelian.' I said it only to comfort the simple-minded creature; in reality they would have laughed in my face for even thinking to sell such a miserable, ragged thing.

" 'And I thought that they might give a little more, Astafi Ivanich. It is made of cloth, so how is it that they would not wish to pay more than three rubles for it?'

" 'Well, Emelian, if you wish to sell it, then of course you may ask more for it at first.'

"Emelian was silent for a moment, then he once more called to me.

" 'Astafi Ivanich!'

" 'What is it, Emelian?'

" 'You will sell the cloak after I am no more; no need of burying me in it, I can well get along without it; it is worth something, and may come handy to you.'

"Here I felt such a painful gripping at my heart as I can not even express, sir. I saw that the sadness of approaching death had already come upon the man. Again we were silent for some time. About an hour passed in this way. I looked at him again and saw that he was still gazing at me, and when his eyes met mine he immediately lowered his.

" 'Would you like a drink of cold water?' I asked him.

" 'Give me some, and may God repay you, Astafi Ivanich.'

" 'Would you like anything else, Emelian?'

" 'No, Astafi Ivanich, I do not want anything, but I—'

" 'What?'

" 'You know that—'

" 'What is it you want, Emelian?'

" 'The breeches— You know— It was I who took them—Astafi Ivanich—'

" 'Well,' I said, 'the great God will forgive you, Emelian, poor, unfortunate fellow that you are! Depart in peace.'

"And I had to turn away my head for a moment because grief for the poor devil took my breath away and the tears came in torrents from my eyes.

" 'Astafi Ivanich!—'

"I looked at him, saw that he wished to tell me something more, tried to raise himself, and was moving his lips— He reddened and looked at me— Suddenly I saw that he began to grow paler and paler; in a moment he fell with his head thrown back, breathed once, and gave his soul into God's keeping."

THE GREAT TRIANGULAR DUEL

By Captain Frederick Marryat

Jack walked up to the boatswain, and, taking off his hat, with the utmost politeness, said to him:

"If I mistake not, Mr. Biggs, your conversation refers to me."

"Very likely it does," replied the boatswain. "Liseners hear no good of themselves."

"It happears that gentlemen can't converse without being vatched," continued Mr. Easthupp, pulling up his shirt-collar.

"It is not the first time you have thought proper to make very offensive remarks, Mr. Biggs; and as you appear to consider yourself ill-treated in the affair of the trousers, for I tell you at once that it was I who brought them on board, I can only say," continued our hero, with a very polite bow, "that I shall be most happy to give you satisfaction."

"I am your superior officer, Mr. Easy," replied the boatswain.

"Yes, by the rules of the service; but you just now asserted that you would waive your rank: indeed, I dispute it on this occasion; I am on the quarter-deck, and you are not."

"This is the gentleman whom you have insulted, Mr. Easy," replied the boatswain, pointing to the purser's steward.

"Yes, Mr. Heasy, quite as good a gentleman as

126

yourself, altho I 'ave 'ad misfortunes. I ham of as hold a family as hany in the country," replied Mr. Easthupp, now backed by the boatswain. "Many the year did I valk Bond Street, and I 'ave as good blood in my weins as you, Mr. Heasy, altho I 'ave been misfortunate. I've had hadmirals in my family."

"You have grossly insulted this gentleman," said Mr. Biggs, in continuation; "and, notwithstanding all your talk of equality, you are afraid to give him satisfaction; you shelter yourself under your quarter-deck."

"Mr. Biggs," replied our hero, who was now very wroth, "I shall go on shore directly we arrive at Malta. Let you, and this fellow, put on plain clothes, and I will meet you both; and then I will show you whether I am afraid to give satisfaction."

"One at a time," said the boatswain.

"No, sir, not one at a time, but both at the same time, I will fight both or none. If you are my superior officer, you must descend," replied Jack, with an ironical sneer, "to meet me, or I will not descend to meet that fellow, whom I believe to have been little better than a pickpocket." . . .

Mr. Biggs, having declared he would fight, of course had to look out for a second, and he fixed upon Mr. Tallboys, the gunner, and requested him to be his friend. Mr. Tallboys, who had been latterly very much annoyed by Jack's victories over him in the science of navigation, and therefore felt ill-will toward him, consented; but he was very much puzzled how to arrange that three were to fight at the same time, for he had no idea of there being two duels; so he went to his cabin and commenced read-

ing. Jack, on the other hand, daring not say a word
to Jolliffe on the subject; indeed, there was no one
in the ship to whom he could confide but Gascoigne;
he therefore went to him, and, altho Gascoigne
thought it was excessively infra dig. of Jack to meet
even the boatswain; as the challenge had been given,
there was no retracting, and he therefore consented,
like all midshipmen, anticipating fun, and quite
thoughtless of the consequences. . . .

Mr. Tallboys addressed Mr. Gascoigne, taking him
apart while the boatswain amused himself with a
glass of grog, and our hero sat outside, teasing a
monkey.

"Mr. Gascoigne," said the gunner, "I have been
very much puzzled how this duel should be fought,
but I have at last found out. You see there are
three parties to fight; had there been two or four
there would have been no difficulty, as the right line
or square might guide us in that instance; but we
must arrange it upon the triangle in this."

Gascoigne stared: he could not imagine what was
coming.

"Are you aware, Mr. Gascoigne, of the properties
of an equilateral triangle?"

"Yes," replied the midshipman; "it has three equal
sides. But what the devil has that to do with the
duel?"

"Everything, Mr. Gascoigne," replied the gunner;
"it has resolved the great difficulty; indeed, the duel
between three can only be fought upon that principle.
You observe," said the gunner, taking a piece of
chalk out of his pocket and making a triangle on the
table, "in this figure we have three points, each equi-
distant from each other; and we have three combat-

ants; so that placing one at each point, it is all fair play for the three: Mr. Easy, for instance, stands here, the boatswain here, and the purser's steward at the third corner. Now, if the distance is fairly measured, it will be all right."

"But then," replied Gascoigne, delighted at the idea, "how are they to fire?"

"It certainly is not of much consequence," replied the gunner; "but still, as sailors, it appears to me that they should fire with the sun; that is, Mr. Easy fires at Mr. Biggs, Mr. Biggs at Mr. Easthupp, and Mr. Easthupp fires at Mr. Easy, so that you perceive that each party has his shot at one, and at the same time receives the fire of another."

Gascoigne was in ecstasies at the novelty of the proceeding, the more so as he perceived that Easy obtained every advantage of the arrangement.

"Upon my word, Mr. Tallboys, I give you great credit; you have a profound mathematical head, and I am delighted with your arrangement. Of course, in these affairs the principals are bound to comply with the arrangements of the seconds, and I shall insist upon Mr. Easy consenting to your excellent and scientific proposal."

Gascoigne went out, and, pulling Jack away from the monkey, told him what the gunner had proposed, at which Jack laughed heartily.

The gunner also explained it to the boatswain, who did not very well comprehend, but replied:

"I dare say it's all right, shot for shot, and damn all favors."

The parties then repaired to the spot with two pairs of ship's pistols, which Mr. Tallboys had smuggled on shore; and as soon as they were on the ground the gunner called Mr. Easthupp out of the cooperage. In the meantime Gascoigne had been measuring an equilateral triangle of twelve paces, and marked it out. Mr. Tallboys, on his return with the purser's steward, went over the ground, and, finding that it was "equal angles subtended by equal sides," declared that all was right. Easy took his station, the boatswain was put into his, and Mr. Easthupp, who was quite in a mystery, was led by the gunner to the third position.

"But, Mr. Tallboys," said the purser's steward, "I don't understand this. Mr. Easy will first fight Mr. Biggs, will he not?"

"No," replied the gunner, "this is a duel of three. You will fire at Mr. Easy, Mr. Easy will fire at Mr. Biggs, and Mr. Biggs will fire at you. It is all arranged, Mr. Easthupp."

"But," said Mr. Easthupp, "I do not understand it. Why is Mr. Biggs to fire at me? I have no quarrel with Mr. Biggs."

"Because Mr. Easy fires at Mr. Biggs, and Mr. Biggs must have his shot as well."

"If you have ever been in the company of gentlemen, Mr. Easthupp," observed Gascoigne, "you must know something about duelling."

"Yes, yes, I've kept the best company, Mr. Gascoigne, and I can give a gentleman satisfaction; but——"

"Then, sir, if that is the case, you must know that your honor is in the hands of your second, and that no gentleman appeals."

"Yes, yes, I know that, Mr. Gascoigne; but, still, I've no quarrel with Mr. Biggs, and therefore Mr. Biggs, of course, will not aim at me."

"Why, you don't think that I'm going to be fired at for nothing?" replied the boatswain. "No, no, I'll have my shot anyhow."

"But at your friend, Mr. Biggs?"

"All the same I shall fire at somebody; shot for shot, and hit the luckiest."

"Vel, gentlemen, I purtest against these proceedings," replied Mr. Easthupp. "I came here to have satisfaction from Mr. Easy, and not to be fired at by Mr. Biggs."

"Don't you have satisfaction when you fire at Mr. Easy?" replied the gunner. "What more would you have?"

"I purtest against Mr. Biggs firing at me."

"So you would have a shot without receiving one!" cried Gascoigne. "The fact is that this fellow's a confounded coward, and ought to be kicked into the cooperage again."

At this affront Mr. Easthupp rallied, and accepted the pistol offered by the gunner.

"You 'ear those words, Mr. Biggs? Pretty language to use to a gentleman! You shall 'ear from me, sir, as soon as the ship is paid off. I purtest no longer, Mr. Tallboys. Death before dishonor! I'm a gentleman, damme!"

At all events, the swell was not a very courageous gentleman, for he trembled most exceedingly as he pointed his pistol. The gunner gave the word as if he were exercising the great guns on board ship.

"Cock your locks! Take good aim at the object! Fire! Stop your vents!"

The only one of the combatants who appeared to comply with the latter supplementary order was Mr. Easthupp, who clapped his hand to his trousers behind, gave a loud yell, and then dropped down, the bullet having passed clean through his seat of honor, from his having presented his broadside as a target to the boatswain as he faced toward our hero. Jack's shot had also taken effect, having passed through both the boatswain's cheeks, without further mischief than extracting two of his best upper double teeth and forcing through the hole of the further cheek the boatswain's own quid of tobacco. As for Mr. Easthupp's ball, as he was very unsettled, and shut his eyes before he fired, it had gone the Lord knows where.

The purser's steward lay on the ground and screamed; the boatswain spit out his double teeth and two or three mouthfuls of blood, and then threw down his pistol in a rage.

"A pretty business, by God!" sputtered he. "He's put my pipe out. How the devil am I to pipe to dinner when I'm ordered, all my wind 'scaping through the cheeks?"

In the meantime, the others had gone to the assistance of the purser's steward, who continued his vociferations. They examined him, and considered a wound in that part not to be dangerous.

"Hold your confounded bawling," cried the gunner, "or you'll have the guard down here. You've not hurt."

"Hain't hi!" roared the steward. "Oh, let me die! Let me die! Don't move me!"

"Nonsense!" cried the gunner, "you must get up and walk down to the boat; if you don't, we'll leave you. Hold your tongue, confound you! You won't? Then I'll give you something to halloo for."

Whereupon Mr. Tallboys commenced cuffing the

poor wretch right and left, who received so many swinging boxes of the ear that he was soon reduced to merely pitiful plaints of "Oh, dear! such inhumanity! I purtest! Oh, dear! must I get up? I can't, indeed."

"I do not think he can move, Mr. Tallboys," said Gascoigne. "I should think the best plan would be to call up two of the men from the cooperage and let them take him at once to the hospital."

The gunner went down to the cooperage to call the men. Mr. Biggs, who had bound up his face as if he had a toothache, for the bleeding had been very slight, came up to the purser's steward, exclaiming:

"What the hell are you making such a howling about? Look at me, with two shot-holes through my figurehead, while you have only got one in your stern. I wish I could change with you, by heavens! for I could use my whistle then. Now, if I attempt to pipe, there will be such a wasteful expenditure of his Majesty's store of wind that I never shall get out a note. A wicked shot of yours, Mr. Easy."

"I really am very sorry," replied Jack, with a polite bow, "and I beg to offer my best apology."

—*"Midshipman Easy."*

THE PASSAGE OF THE RED SEA

By Henri Murger

For five or six years Marcel had been engaged upon the famous painting which he said was meant to represent the Passage of the Red Sea; and for five or six years this masterpiece in color had been obstinately refused by the jury. Indeed, from its constant journeying back and forth, from the artist's studio to the Musée, and from the Musée to the studio, the painting knew the road so well that one needed only to set it on rollers and it would have been quite capable of reaching the Louvre alone. Marcel, who had repainted the picture ten times, and minutely gone over it from top to bottom, vowed that only a personal hostility on the part of the members of the jury could account for the ostracism which annually turned him away from the Salon, and in his idle moments he had composed, in honor of those watch-dogs of the Institute, a little dictionary of insults, with illustrations of a savage irony. This collection gained celebrity and enjoyed, among the studios and in the Ecole des Beaux-Arts, the same sort of popular success as that achieved by the immortal complaint of Giovanni Bellini, painter by appointment to the Grand Sultan of the Turks; every dauber in Paris had a copy stored away in his memory.

For a long time Marcel had not allowed himself to

be discouraged by the emphatic refusal which greeted
him at each exposition. He was comfortably settled
in his opinion that his picture was, in a modest way,
the companion piece long awaited by the "Wedding of
Cana," that gigantic masterpiece whose dazzling splen-
dor the dust of three centuries has not dimmed. Accordingly, each year, at the time of the Salon, Marcel
sent his picture to be examined by the jury. Only, in
order to throw the examiners off the track and if possible to make them abandon the policy of exclusion
which they seemed to have adopted toward the "Passage of the Red Sea," Marcel, without in any way dis-
turbing the general scheme of his picture, modified
certain details and changed its title.

For instance, on one occasion it arrived before the
jury under the name of the "Passage of the Rubicon!"
but Pharaoh, poorly disguised under Caesar's mantle,
was recognized and repulsed with all the honors that
were his due.

The following year, Marcel spread over the level
plane of his picture a layer of white representing snow,
planted a pine-tree in one corner, and clothing an
Egyptian as a grenadier of the Imperial Guard, re-
christened the painting the "Passage of the Beresina."

The jury, which on that very day had polished its
spectacles on the lining of its illustrious coat, was not
in any way taken in by this new ruse. It recognized
perfectly well the persistent painting, above all by a
big brute of a horse of many colors, which was rearing out of one of the waves of the Red Sea. The coat
of that horse had served Marcel for all his experiments
in color, and in private conversation he called it his
synoptic table of fine tones, because he had repro-
duced, in their play of light and shade, all possible com-

binations of color. But once again, insensible to this detail, the jury seemed scarcely able to find black-balls enough to emphasize their refusal of the "Passage of the Beresina."

"Very well," said Marcel; "no more than I expected. Next year I shall send it back under the title of 'Passage des Panoramas.' "

"That will be one on them—on them—on them, them, them," sang the musician, Schaunard, fitting the words to a new air he had been composing—a terrible air, noisy as a gamut of thunderclaps, and the accompaniment to which was a terror to every piano in the neighborhood.

"How could they refuse that picture without having every drop of the vermilion in my Red Sea rise up in their faces and cover them with shame?" murmured Marcel, as he gazed at the painting. "When one thinks that it contains a good hundred crowns' worth of paint, and a million of genius, not to speak of the fair days of my youth, fast growing bald as my hat! But they shall never have the last word; until my dying breath I shall keep on sending them my painting. I want to have it engraved upon their memory."

"That is certainly the surest way of ever getting it engraved," said Gustave Colline, in a plaintive voice, adding to himself: "That was a good one, that was—really a good one; I must get that off the next time I am asked out."

Marcel continued his imprecations, which Schaunard continued to set to music.

"Oh, they won't accept me," said Marcel. "Ah! the government pays them, boards them, gives them the Cross, solely for the one purpose of refusing me once a year, on the 1st of March. I see their idea clearly now—I see it perfectly clearly; they are trying to drive me to break my brushes. They hope, perhaps, by refusing my Red Sea, to make me throw myself out of the window in despair. But they know very little of the human heart if they expect to catch me with such a clumsy trick. I shall no longer wait for the time of the annual Salon. Beginning with to-day, my work becomes the canvas of Damocles, eternally suspended over their existence. From now on, I am going to send it once a week to each one of them, at their homes, in the bosom of their families, in the full heart of their private life. It shall trouble their domestic joy, it shall make them think that their wine is sour, their dinner burned, their wives bad-tempered. They will very soon become insane, and will have to be put in strait-jackets when they go to the Insitute, on the days when there are meetings. That idea pleases me."

A few days later, when Marcel had already forgotten his terrible plans for vengeance upon his persecutors, he received a visit from Father Medicis. For that was the name by which the brotherhood called a certain Jew, whose real name was Soloman, and who at that time was well known throughout the bohemia of art and literature, with which he constantly had dealings. Father Medicis dealt in all sorts of bric-à-brac. He sold complete house-furnishings for from twelve francs up to a thousand crowns. He would buy anything, and knew how to sell it again at a profit. His shop, situated in the Place du Carrousel, was a fairy spot where one could find everything that one might wish. All the products of nature, all the creations of art, all that comes forth from the bowels of the earth or from the genius of man, Medicis found it profitable to trade in. His dealings included everything, absolutely

everything that exists; he even put a price upon the
Ideal. Medicis would even buy ideas, to use himself
or to sell again. Known to all writers and artists,
intimate friend of the palette, familiar spirit of the
writing-desk, he was the Asmodeus of the arts. He
would sell you cigars in exchange for the plot of a
dime novel, slippers for a sonnet, a fresh catch of fish
for a paradox; he would talk at so much an hour
with newspaper reporters whose duty was to record
the lively capers of the smart set. He would get you
passes to the parliament buildings, or invitations to
private parties; he gave lodgings by the night, the
week, or the month to homeless artists, who paid him
by making copies of old masters in the Louvre. The
greenroom had no secrets for him; he could place your
plays for you with some manager; he could obtain
for you all sorts of favors. He carried in his head a
copy of the almanac of twenty-five thousand ad-
dresses, and knew the residence, the name, and the
secrets of all the celebrities, even the obscure ones.

In entering the abode of the bohemians, with that
knowing air which characterized him, the Jew divined
that he had arrived at a propitious moment. As a
matter of fact, the four friends were at that moment
gathered in council, and under the domination of a
ferocious appetite were discussing the grave question
of bread and meat. It was Sunday, the last day of
the month. Fatal day, sinister of date!

The entrance of Medicis was accordingly greeted
with a joyous chorus, for they knew that the Jew was
too avaricious of his time to waste it in mere visits of
civility; accordingly his presence always announced
that he was open to a bargain.

"Good evening, gentlemen," said the Jew; "how are you?"

"Colline," said Rodolphe from where he lay upon the bed, sunk in the delights of maintaining a horizontal line, "practise the duties of hospitality and offer our guest a chair; a guest is sacred. I salute you, Abraham," added the poet.

Colline drew forward a chair which had about as much elasticity as a piece of bronze and offered it to the Jew. Medicis let himself fall into the chair, and started to complain of its hardness, when he remembered that he himself had once traded it off to Colline in exchange for a profession of faith which he afterward sold to a deputy. As he sat down the pockets of the Jew gave forth a silvery sound, and this melodious symphony threw the four bohemians into a reverie that was full of sweetness.

"Now," said Rodolphe, in a low tone, to Marcel, "let us hear the song. The accompaniment sounds all right."

"Monsieur Marcel," said Medicis. "I have simply come to make your fortune. That is to say, I have come to offer you a superb opportunity to enter into the world of art. Art, as you very well know, Monsieur Marcel, is an arid road, in which glory is the oasis."

"Father Medicis," said Marcel, who was on coals of impatience, "in the name of fifty per cent, your revered patron saint, be brief."

"Here is the offer," rejoined Medicis. "A wealthy amateur, who is collecting a picture-gallery destined to make the tour of Europe, has commissioned me to procure for him a series of remarkable works. I have come to give you a chance to be included in this collection. In one word, I have come to purchase your 'Passage of the Red Sea.'"

"Money down?" asked Marcel.

"Money down," answered the Jew, sounding forth the full orchestra of his pockets.

"Go on, Medicis," said Marcel, pointing to his painting. "I wish to leave to you the honor of fixing for yourself the price of that work of art which is priceless."

The Jew laid upon the table fifty crowns in bright new silver.

"Keep them going," said Marcel; "that is a good beginning."

"Monsieur Marcel," said Medicis, "you know very well that my first word is always my last word. I shall add nothing more. But think; fifty crowns; that makes one hundred and fifty francs. That is quite a sum."

"A paltry sum," answered the artist; "just in the robe of my Pharaoh there is fifty crowns' worth of cobalt. Pay me at least something for my work."

"Hear my last word," replied Medicis. "I will not add a penny more; but, I offer dinner for the crowd, wines included, and after dessert I will pay in gold."

"Do I hear any one object?" howled Colline, striking three blows of his fist upon the table. "It is a bargain."

"Come on," said Marcel. "I agree."

"I will send for the picture to-morrow," said the Jew. "Come, gentlemen, let us start. Your places are all set."

The four friends descended the stairs, singing the chorus from "The Huguenots," "to the table, to the table."

Medicis treated the bohemians in a fashion altogether sumptuous. He offered them a lot of things which up to now had remained for them a mystery. Dating from this dinner, lobster ceased to be a myth to Schaunard, and he acquired a passion for that amphibian which was destined to increase to the verge of delirium.

The four friends went forth from this splendid feast as intoxicated as on a day of vintage. Their inebriety came near bearing deplorable fruits for Marcel, because as he passed the shop of his tailor, at two o'clock in the morning, he absolutely insisted upon awakening his creditor in order to give him, on account, the one hundred and fifty francs that he had just received. But a gleam of reason still awake in the brain of Colline held back the artist from the brink of this precipice.

A week after this festivity Marcel learned in what gallery his picture had found a place. Passing along the Faubourg Saint-Honoré, he stopped in the midst of a crowd that seemed to be staring at a sign newly placed above a shop. This sign was none other than Marcel's painting, which had been sold by Medicis to a dealer in provisions. Only the "Passage of the Red Sea" had once again undergone a modification and bore a new title. A steamboat had been added to it, and it was now called "In the Port of Marseilles." A flattering ovation arose among the crowd when they discovered the picture. And Marcel turned away delighted with this triumph, and murmured softly: "The voice of the people is the voice of God!"

THE MAN FROM RED DOG

By ALFRED HENRY LEWIS

"Let me try one of them thar seegyars."

It was the pleasant after-dinner hour, and I was on the veranda for a quiet smoke. The Old Cattleman had just thrown down his paper; the half-light of the waning sun was a bit too dim for his eyes of seventy years.

"Whenever I behold a seegyar," said the old fellow, as he puffed voluminously at the principe I passed over, "I thinks of what that witness says in the murder trial at Socorro.

" 'What was you-all doin' in camp yourse'f,' asked the jedge of this yere witness, 'the day of the killin'?'

" 'Which,' says the witness, oncrossin' his laigs an' lettin' on he ain't made bashful an' oneasy by so much attentions bein' shown him, 'which I was a-eatin' of a few sardines, a-drinkin' of a few drinks of whisky, a-smokin' of a few seegyars, an' a-romancin' 'round.' "

After this abrupt, not to say ambiguous reminiscence, the Old Cattleman puffed contentedly a moment.

"What murder trial was this you speak of?" I asked. "Who had been killed?"

"Now I don't reckon I ever does know who it is gets downed," he replied. "This yere murder trial itse'f is news to me complete. They was waggin' along with it when I trails into Socorro that time, an' I

merely sa'nters over to the co't that a-way to hear
what's goin' on. The jedge is sorter gettin' in on the
play while I'm listenin'.

" 'What was the last words of this yere gent who's
killed?' asked the jedge of this witness.

" 'As nearly as I keeps tabs, jedge,' says the witness, 'the dyin' statement of this person is: "Four aces
to beat." '

" 'Which if deceased had knowed Socorro like I
does,' says the jedge, like he's commentin' to himse'f,
'he'd shorely realized that sech remarks is simply sooi-
cidal.' "

Again the Old Cattleman relapsed into silence and
the smoke of the principe.

"How did the trial come out?" I queried. "Was
the accused found guilty?"

"Which the trial itse'f," he replied, "don't come out.
Thar's a passel of the boys who's come into town to
see that jestice is done, an' bein' the round-up is goin'
for'ard at the time, they nacherally feels hurried an'
pressed for leesure. They-alls oughter be back on the
range with their cattle. So the fifth day, when things
is loiterin' along at the trial till it looks like the law
has hobbles on, an' the word goes round it's goin' to be
a week yet before the jury gets action on this mis-
creant who's bein' tried, the boys becomes plumb aggravated an' wearied out that a-way; an', kickin' in the
door of the calaboose, they searches out the felon,
swings him to a cottonwood not otherwise engaged, an'
the right prevails. Nacherally the trial bogs down right
thar."

After another season of silence and smoke, the Old
Cattleman struck in again.

"Speakin' of killin's, while I'm the last gent to go

fosterin' idees of bloodshed, I'm some discouraged jest now by what I've been readin' in that paper about a dooel between some Eytalians, an' it shorely tries me the way them aliens plays hoss. It's obvious as stars on a cl'ar night, they never means fight a little bit. I abhors dooels, an' cowers from the mere idee. But, after all, business is business, an' when folks fights 'em the objects of the meetin' oughter be blood. But the way these yere European shorthorns fixes it, a gent shorely runs a heap more resk of becomin' a angel abrupt, attendin' of a Texas cake-walk in a purely social way.

"Do they ever fight dooels in the West? Why, yes —some. My mem'ry comes a canterin' up right now with the details of an encounter I once beholds in Wolfville. Thar ain't no time much throwed away with a dooel in the Southwest. The people's mighty extemporaneous, an' don't go browsin' 'round none sendin' challenges in writin', an' that sort of flapdoodle. When a gent notices the signs a-gettin' about right for him to go on the war-path, he picks out his meat, surges up, an' declar's himse'f. The victim, who is most likely a mighty serious an' experienced person, don't copper the play by makin' vain remarks, but brings his gatlin' into play surprizin'. Next it's bang! bang! bang! mixed up with flashes an' white smoke, an' the dooel is over complete. The gent who still adorns our midst takes a drink on the house, while St. Peter onbars things a lot an' arranges gate an' seat checks with the other in the realms of light. That's all thar is to it. The tide of life ag'in flows onward to the eternal sea, an' nary ripple.

"Oh, this yere Wolfville dooel! Well, it's this a-way. The day is blazin' hot, an' business layin' prone

an' dead—jest blistered to death. A passel of us is
sorter pervadin' round the dance-hall, it bein' the big-
gest an' coolest store in camp. A monte game is strug-
glin' for breath in a feeble, fitful way in a corner, an'
some of us is a-watchin'; an' some a-settin' 'round
loose a-thinkin'; but all keepin' mum an' still, 'cause
it's so hot.

"Jest then some gent on a hoss goes whoopin' up
the street a-yellin' an' a-whirlin' the loop of his rope,
an' allowin' generally he's havin' a mighty good time.

" 'Who's this yere toomultuous man on the hoss?'
says Enright, a-regardin' of him in a displeased way
from the door.

" 'I meets him up the street a minute back,' says
Dan Boggs, 'an' he allows he's called "The Man from
Red Dog." He says he's took a day off to visit us,
an' aims to lay waste the camp some before he goes
back.'

"About then the Red Dog man notes old Santa Rosa,
who keeps the Mexican *baile* hall, an' his old woman,
Marie, a-fussin' with each other in front of the New
York Store. They's locked horns over a drink or
somethin', an' is pow-wowin' mighty onamiable.

" 'Whatever does this yere Mexican fam'ly mean,'
says the Red Dog man, a-surveyin' of 'em plenty
scornful, 'a-draggin' of their domestic brawls out yere
to offend a sufferin' public for? Whyever don't they
stay in their wickeyup an' fight, an' not take to puttin' it all over the American race which ain't in the
play none an' don't thirst tharfor? However, I unites
an' reconciles this divided household easy.'

"With this the Red Dog man drops the loop of his
lariat 'round the two contestants an' jumps his bronco
up the street like it's come outen a gun. Of course

Santa Rosa an' Marie goes along on their heads per-
miscus.

"They goes coastin' along ontil they gets pulled into
a mesquite-bush, an' the rope slips offen the saddle,
an' thar they be. We-alls goes over from the dance-
hall, extricatin' of 'em, an' final they round up mighty
hapless an' weak, an' can only walk. They shorely
lose enough hide to make a pair of leggin's.

" 'Which I brings 'em together like twins,' says the
Red Dog man, ridin' back for his rope. 'I offers two
to one, no limit, they don't fight none whatever for a
month.'

"Which, as it shorely looks like he's right, no one
takes him. So the Red Dog man leaves his bluff a-
hangin' an' goes into the dance-hall, a-givin' of it out
cold an' clammy he meditates libatin'.

" 'All promenade to the bar,' yells the Red Dog
man as he goes in. 'I'm a wolf, an' it's my night to
howl. Don't 'rouse me, barkeep, with the sight of
merely one bottle; set 'em all up. I'm some fas-
tidious about my fire-water an' likes chance to select.'

"Well, we-alls takes our inspiration, an' the Red
Dog man tucks his onder his belt an' then turns
round to Enright.

" 'I takes it your'e the old he-coon of this yere
outfit?' says the Red Dog man, soopercilious-like.

" 'Which, if I ain't,' says Enright, 'it's plenty safe as
a play to let your wisdom flow this a-way till the
he-coon gets yere.'

" 'If that's anythin',' says the Red Dog man, 'I
turns from sick, it's voylence an' deevastation. But
I hears such complaints constant of this yere camp
of Wolfville, I takes my first idle day to ride over
an' line things up. Now yere I be, an' while I re-

grets it, I finds you-alls is a lawless, onregenerate set, a heap sight worse than roomer. I now takes the notion—for I sees no other trail—that by next drink time I climbs into the saddle, throws my rope 'round this den of sin, an' removes it from the map.'

"'Nacherally,' says Enright, some sarcastic, 'in makin' them schemes you ain't lookin' for no trouble whatever with a band of terrapins like us.'

"'None whatever,' says the Red Dog man, mighty confident. 'In thirty minutes I distributes this yere hamlet 'round in the landscape same as them Greasers; which feat becomin' hist'ry, I then canters back to Red Dog.'

"'Well,' says Enright, 'it's plenty p'lite to let us know what's comin' this a-way.'

"'Oh! I ain't tellin' you none,' says the Red Dog man, 'I simply lets fly this hint, so any of you-alls as has got bric-à-brac he values speshul, he takes warnin' some an' packs it off all safe.'

"It's about then when Cherokee Hall, who's lookin' on, shoulders in between Enright an' the Red Dog man, mighty positive. Cherokee is a heap sot in his idees, an' I sees right off he's took a notion ag'in the Red Dog man.

"'As you've got a lot of work cut out,' says Cherokee, eyein' the Red Dog man malignant, 's'pose we tips the canteen ag'in.'

"'I shorely goes you,' says the Red Dog man. 'I drinks with friend, an' I drinks with foe; with the pard of my bosom an' the shudderin' victim of my wrath all sim'lar.'

"Cherokee turns out a big drink an' stands a-holdin' of it in his hand. I wants to say right yere, this Cherokee's plenty guileful.

" 'You was namin',' says Cherokee, 'some public improvements you aims to make; sech as movin' this yere camp 'round some, I believes?'

" 'That's whatever,' says the Red Dog man, 'an' the holycaust I 'nitiates is due to start in fifteen minutes.'

" 'I've been figgerin' on you,' says Cherokee, 'an' I gives you the result in strict confidence without holdin' out a kyard. When you-all talks of tearin' up Wolfville, you're a liar an' hoss-thief, an' you ain't goin' to tear up nothin'.'

" 'What's this I hears!' yells the frenzied Red Dog man, reachin' for his gun.

"But he never gets it, for the same second Cherokee spills the glass of whisky straight in his eyes, an' the next he's anguished an' blind as a mole.

" 'I'll fool this yere human simoon up a lot,' says Cherokee, a-hurlin' of the Red Dog man to the floor, face down, while his nine-inch bowie shines in his hand like the sting of a wasp. 'I shore fixes him so he can't get a job clerkin' in a store,' an' grabbin' the Red Dog man's ha'r, which is long as the mane of a pony, he slashes it off close in one motion.

" 'Thar's a fringe for your leggin's, Nell,' remarks Cherokee, a-turnin' of the crop over to Faro Nell. 'Now, Doc,' Cherokee goes on to Doc Peets, 'take this yere Red Dog stranger over to the Red Light, fix his eyes all right, an' then tell him, if he thinks he needs blood in this, to take his Winchester an' go north in the middle of the street. In twenty minutes by the watch I steps outen the dance-hall door a-lookin' for him. P'int him to the door all fair an' squar'. I don't aim to play nothin' low on this yere gent. He gets a chance for his ante.'

"Doc Peets sorter accoomilates the Red Dog man,
who is cussin' an' carryin' on scand'lous, an' leads
him over to the Red Light. In a minute word
comes to Cherokee as his eyes is roundin' up all
proper, an' that he's makin' war-medicine an' is
growin' more hostile constant, an' to heel himse'f.
At that Cherokee, mighty ca'm, sends out for Jack
Moore's Winchester, which is an 'eight-squar',' latest
model.

"'Oh, Cherokee!' says Faro Nell, beginnin' to cry,
an' curlin' her arms 'round his neck. I'm 'fraid he's
goin' to down you. Ain't thar no way to fix it?
Can't Dan yere settle with this Red Dog man?'

"'Cert,' says Dan Boggs, 'an' I makes the trip
too gleeful. Jest to spar' Nell's feelin's, Cherokee,
an' not to interfere with no gent's little game, I takes
your hand an' plays it.'

"'Not none,' says Cherokee; 'this is my deal.
Don't cry, Nellie,' he adds, smoothin' down her yaller
ha'r. 'Folks in my business has to hold themse'fs
ready to face any game on the word, an' they never
weakens or lays down. An' another thing, little girl;
I gets this Red Dog sharp shore. I'm in the middle
of a run of luck; I holds fours twice last night, with
a flush an' a full hand out ag'in 'em.'

"Nell at last lets go of Cherokee's neck, an', bein'
a female an' timid that a-way, allows she'll go, an'
won't stop to see the shootin' none. We applauds the
idee, thinkin' she might shake Cherokee some if she
stays; an' of course a gent out shootin' for his life
needs his nerve.

"Well, the twenty minutes is up; the Red Dog
man gets his rifle offen his saddle an' goes down the
middle of the street. Turnin' up his big sombrero, he

squar's 'round, cocks his gun, an' waits. Then Enright goes out with Cherokee an' stands him in the street about a hundred yards from the Red Dog man. After Cherokee's placed he holds up his hand for attention an' says:

"'When all is ready I stands to one side an' drops my hat. You-alls fires at will.'

"Enright goes over to the side of the street, counts 'one,' 'two,' 'three,' an' drops his hat. Bangety! Bang! Bang! goes the rifles like the roll of a drum. Cherokee can work a Winchester like one of these yere Yankee 'larm-clocks, an' that Red Dog hold-up don't seem none behind.

"About the fifth fire the Red Dog man sorter steps for'ard an' drops his gun; an' after standin' onsteady for a second, he starts to cripplin' down at his knees. At last he comes ahead on his face like a landside. Thar's two bullets plum through his lungs, an' when we gets to him the red froth is comin' outen his mouth some plenteous.

"We packs him back into the Red Light an' lays him onto a monte-table. Bimeby he comes to a little an' Peets asks him whatever he thinks he wants.

"'I wants you-alls to take off my moccasins an' pack me into the street,' says the Red Dog man. 'I ain't allowin' for my old mother in Missoury to be told as how I dies in no gin-mill, which she shorely 'bominates of 'em. An' I don't die with no boots on, neither.'

"We-alls packs him back into the street ag'in, an' pulls away at his boots. About the time we gets 'em off he sags back convulsive, an' thar he is as dead as Santa Anna.

"'What sort of a game is this, anyhow?' says

Dan Boggs, who, while we stands thar, has been pawin' over the Red Dog man's rifle. 'Looks like this vivacious party's plumb locoed. Yere's his hind-sights wedged up for a thousand yards, an' he's been a-shootin' of cartridges with a hundred an' twenty grains of powder into 'em. Between the sights an' the jump of the powder, he's shootin' plumb over Cherokee an' aimin' straight at him.'

" 'Nellie,' says Enright, lookin' remorseful at the girl, who colors up an' begins to cry ag'in, 'did you cold-deck this yere Red Dog sport this a-way?'

" 'I'm 'fraid,' sobs Nell, 'he gets Cherokee; so I slides over when you-alls is waitin' an' fixes his gun some.'

" 'Which I should shorely concede you did,' says Enright. 'The way that Red Dog gent manip'lates his weepon shows he knows his game; an' except for you a-settin' things up on him, I'm powerful afraid he'd spoiled Cherokee a whole lot.'

" 'Well, gents,' goes on Enright, after thinkin' a while, 'I reckon we-alls might as well drink on it. Hist'ry never shows a game yet, an' a woman in it, which is on the squar', an' we meekly b'ars our burdens with the rest.' "

BOPPO'S BICYCLE

By James Warner Bellah

His name was George Stanley St. Anselme Stokes-Mowbray. His father was a brigadier. His uncle was a bishop. His brother was a first secretary and his sister wore flat heels and wrote frightful novels of the Midlands. At the age of ten George Stanley gave up trying and settled into the career of disgracing his family.

They seemed to realize from the beginning that a duck had been hatched in their midst. They conferred and sent him to school in Belgium until his attitude should change.

At eighteen they knew the worst. It would never change. George Stanley was a blot and a mistake. In a year or so—India, Hongkong, Egypt and exit George Stanley forever from the pompous dignified hearths of the righteous Stokes-Mowbrays.

All very well and quite proper save for the fact that on the afternoon of the 4th of August, 1914, George Stanley was stopped near Liége at the point of a bayonet and told to get off his bicycle.

"But, see here," said George Stanley, "have a peek at my jolly old passport?"

The man with the bayonet shook his head, grasped the handlebars of the wheel, vaulted into the saddle and pedaled furiously down the road.

George Stanley stood quite still and stared after him for a moment until the solution of the difficulty came to him. "I say, you silly ass!" he shouted, "I shall have you arrested for this, y' know." There was no answer, and presently the man was out of sight. George Stanley removed his cycling cap and scratched the crown of his head with his middle finger. He turned around and stared in the opposite direction. Nothing. He sat down at the side of the road and pulled a bar of milk chocolate from his pocket. Presently he lit his pipe and sprawled back upon the grass.

Perhaps an hour later he sat up quickly and held out his hand tentatively to catch a raindrop. None fell and yet thunder rumbled threateningly on the distant horizon. Mildly he wondered why no motors had passed to give him a lift. He stood up and stretched languidly. Stupid country where chaps were allowed to wander about stealing bicycles!

He stepped out into the roadway again and stared in both directions. He blinked, and his mouth fell open. Two fields away to the right, lying flat on their stomachs, was a battalion of men in képis with rifles in hand and marching packs strapped to their backs. Beyond them a mile or so away, a huge column of black smoke suddenly rose to a great height, mushroomed slowly and drifted eastward on the summer breeze.

"Hullo," he muttered. "Fireworks, not?"

Vaguely he tried to remember something he felt he ought to know. Again he scratched his head with his middle finger, and his brow puckered in thought. Everything connected up somehow. He was sure of that. If he could only remember just how it con-

nected. Another black pillar of smoke rose into
the air—nearer this time—and again the ground trembled sullenly to the distant crash of thunder. A
bugle screamed across the fields. Some of the men
rose from their stomachs, and there was a broken
flash of light as they whipped long bayonets from their
scabbards and fixed them.

"By Jove," said George Stanley aloud. "That's it!
I knew I'd think of it. It's a war. Read about
it in the papers last night. Stupid Russians fighting
stupid Germans. Stupid Germans fighting stupid Belgians. Ha!" He grinned and pulled his cap vizor
down to shade his eyes. "Splendid seat for the
show, what? Watch it a bit, yes?"

A third pillar of black smoke leaped into the air.
More followed it in quick succession, springing up
in a row like evil jinn, until the blue summer sky
was smudged with soot. The air pulsated constantly
to the distant roar. More men in képis were running across the fields in close formation. Far up
the road, toward the shell bursts, scattered figures
in dark blue appeared in groups of twos and threes.
Some of them tripped and fell and made no effort to
get up again. Suddenly from the fields at the right
a whistle shrieked, and the rippling, whiplash crackle
of rifle fire drowned it out. George Stanley blinked
and sneezed as the burnt powder tickled his nostrils.

"Jolly," he muttered. "What price a pheasant."

Something struck the roadway at his feet and
skipped along like a toad. He leaned down to pick
it up. He whistled in surprise and put his seared
finger to his lips. It was hot. Devilish hot. He
kicked the scrap of metal into the bushes with the
toe of his boot.

"Dangerous," he said. "Chap's liable to get hurt."

More bugles sounded to the left and behind him. He turned to see dark blue clouds of men running across the fields, stooping and tripping as they ran. The scattered groups up the road were coming nearer. Presently a man passed him on the run—wild-eyed and dirty, with his coat fairly torn from his back. Two more men followed him.

"Ho!" yelled George Stanley. "This way! More of your chaps over there." He pointed to the field at the right.

"Sacré nom de nom de nom de bon Dieu!"

"Quite right," said George Stanley. "Perfectly priceless." More stragglers trotted up footsore and weary. An officer with a red band on his arm came sprinting across the fields toward them, shouting and waving his arms. He herded them over the ditch behind the fresh troops, George Stanley with them. He ordered them to lie down and rest.

"But, see here," said George Stanley, "this isn't my jolly show, y' know. Chap pinched my bike— merely waiting for a lift, what?" But the officer was gone again on the run. Once George Stanley started to get up and walk away, but the man nearest to him pulled him back into place and shook his head.

"One has madness! It is the shrapnel!"

Presently the battalion in front rose in a solid wave and trotted forward at the double, stopping every thirty paces to kneel and fire. More stragglers were being herded in from the roadway to join George Stanley's party. There were now almost seventy of them, tired and grimy with caked mud and white dust. They lay in a long row, breathing like exhausted runners—waiting for the next move.

It came quickly and without warning. An officer appeared behind them, pointed to the right and blew his whistle. George Stanley stared and saw blotches of gray-green pushing through the bushes far across the fields.

"Nom de nom encore les allemands!" The tired men crawled forward in an arc to cover the flank and at a second whistle opened fire. The man beside George Stanley fired one round and lay still.

"I say, there," George Stanley shook him, "I say. Have a go at 'em or give me the pea shooter." The man didn't move. George Stanley nudged him again. Still he refused to move. George Stanley inched forward in the line and looked at the man's face.

"Oh, I say," he said softly. "You're dead, what? Sorrow." And he took the rifle.

The gray-green blotches were coming closer. George Stanley watched them push forward pompously, four abreast in column, the ones behind marching steadily onward over the ones in front who had fallen under the first volley. It annoyed him somehow. He squinted through the rifle sights and fired. An officer jumped, threw out his arms and spun face downward into the grass.

"Boppo!" said George Stanley. He nudged the man whose rifle he had taken. "There y' are, Old Tomato, what?"

The fire of the straggler platoon slackened somewhat and men were beginning to hunch up on their elbows and look behind; meanwhile the gray-green blotches trudged steadily on toward them. Somehow George Stanley smelled out what was coming.

"No, y' don't!" he yelled. "You're here now—
stick it. Tirez your blinkin' guns at 'em!" He
waved his arms and fired his own rifle. "See—Boppo!
Comme ci, comme bloomin' ça."

The tired stragglers stared at him dumfounded.
He was standing up now, swinging his arms wildly
over his head. For a moment they hesitated, then
a roar went up. "Vive M'sieur Boppo! A bas les
allemands."

"Quite," said George Stanley. "Precisely what I
was getting at."

Then they lashed out a volley and another and
another. The gray-green blotches hesitated, disin-
tegrated, melted and presently streaked backward toward the far road ditch for cover.

For an hour longer the straggler platoon remained
in the field, then a dusty, bedraggled officer crawled
up behind it and pointed backward. Slowly the
word passed from man to man, and the platoon
inched out of its position and wormed itself back
into the roadway behind. More officers were there,
squatting on their haunches, sweeping the fields with
nervous binoculars. George Stanley touched one of
them upon the elbow.

"I say," he said. "About that jolly old bike of
mine. Some ass pinched it, y' know. Like to have
it back, what?"

The officer stared at him.

"Like to have it back, what?" said George Stanley
somewhat more loudly. The officer turned away
rudely, without speaking. George Stanley stared at
him a moment. "Sorrow," he muttered.

Presently the platoon, scrambling on hands and
knees along the ditch, was headed backward once

more toward Liége. Without thinking much about
it, George Stanley went along.

At nine o'clock that night, after three more skir-
mishes with the gray-green blotches, George Stanley
found himself holding an angle of a stone farmyard
wall some ten miles nearer Liége. He had lost his
cap and thrown away his coat and torn the seat quite
out of his cycling knickerbockers. He was grimy
to the elbows with gun grease and dust and his eyes
were two white flashes in a mask of soot. Further-
more, he was having the first decent time he could
remember—bicycle or no bicycle—since his governess
had come down with measles at Ostend the summer
he was ten years old.

As the night grew colder, he decided that he needed
a coat. He shivered for a few moments in silence
and then crawled quietly around the end of the penthouse and took one from a man who didn't need his
any longer. With the coat he took a képi to replace
his lost cap.

Three times that night Alexander H. R. Von Kluck
tried to break up George Stanley's strong point.
George Stanley didn't know it was *his* strong point,
but he felt vaguely somehow that he ought to hang
onto it for the principle of the thing. So he did—
with the aid of a platoon of nondescript stragglers,
two antiquated mitrailleuses and a half section of
fresh troops that came up around midnight. The
Belgians in the farmyard couldn't see him, but they
could hear him yelling at odd intervals, and when
he yelled they answered him, "Vive M'sieur Boppo!"
and fired more furiously into the crowded darkness
in front. Somehow or other, George Stanley coupled

that darkness with the theft of his bicycle—so he sat
firmly on the little seat of the mitrailleuse and ham-
mered steel-jacketed lead into it. "Priceless, what?"

It began to lighten slowly in front with the cold,
dead grayness of early dawn and a thought began
to trouble George Stanley. He looked backward toward the battered farmhouse across the courtyard.
He looked at his dirty hands and scratched a rib
absently. He beckoned to one of the men to take
his place at the gun. He got up and crawled over
to the doorway. Inside the kitchen, lying on the
floor, he found a young girl and two small children.

"What ho?" he said.

They stirred uneasily, and the girl rose to her knees
whispering excitedly in a steady, rasping, unintelligible
stream of words. George Stanley looked at her, waiting for a break. When it came he said:

"But, I say—what about some warm water, y'
know? Need a bath frightfully, what?"

Apparently she didn't understand, for she went
right on talking. Three times George Stanley tried—
then he crawled disconsolately back into the courtyard. He crouched for a moment, and presently his
eye fell upon the horse trough behind the penthouse.
He was halfway to it when he saw a group of soldiers in the angle of the courtyard wall whispering
and pointing toward him with gesticulations. One
of them detached himself from the group and came
rapidly toward him on hands and knees. He was a
very much smudged and battered staff captain with
orders for the party to retire. Tears ran down his
dirty cheeks. He threw his arms around George
Stanley's shoulders and kissed him. George Stanley
drew back in horror.

"Mon brave!" sobbed the captain. "But it is useless. One must retreat, mon lieutenant."

"Right-o," said George Stanley. "Don't boil over—I'm not your lieutenant."

The staff captain pointed to the insignia on George Stanley's borrowed tunic. "Non—you shall be *captain* for this!"

George Stanley looked curiously at the insignia.

"'Ullo," he said. "Jolly, what? What's it mean?"

"But it is the madness!" exclaimed the captain. "Of a surety it means one is lieutenant."

"Oh—quite," said George Stanley. "But, see here, y' know. Can't jolly well leave this place till I have m' bath, can I? I mean to say—awkward, what? Quite filthy and all that, not?"

The captain shook his head sadly.

"It is the madness." He laid a hand on George Stanley's shoulder. "Mon pauvre M'sieur Boppo. Come." He motioned to the group of men.

Silently they crawled forward, dragging the two machine guns and on hands and knees stole out of the gate in the back wall and down the ditched road, the captain and George Stanley bringing up the rear.

Suddenly George Stanley stopped and sat up on his haunches. With his middle finger he scratched the crown of his head in deep thought. The captain looked at him in amazement and grasped his arm more tightly. Still George Stanley thought on. Then presently his eyes lit up in memory. "That's it," he said. He turned to the captain. "Half a tick Old Onion," he said. "Be with you presently. Just remembered." And before the captain could stop him he was up and running back toward the farm.

The captain tore his hair and called upon four saints in no uncertain tones. He asked le bon Dieu to witness the event and to bring the archangels with him. He told the men to go on with their sergeant while he himself went back after M'sieur the lieutenant Boppo. He went, and presently at a turn in the ditch he met Boppo with two frightened children ahead of him and a very pink-cheeked, misty-eyed girl behind him—crawling along in determined if somewhat awkward procession.

Almost immediately there was a villainous roar behind them and a column of black, greasy smoke sprang up against the dawn sky, carrying the penthouse roof crazily aslant its top. The captain grabbed one child and Boppo the other—and with the girl between them they ran after the rest of the detachment.

It was a long trek back. First of all the captain wasn't quite sure where he was going, and secondly he didn't know whether or not he would find it when he got there. Boppo became more or less annoyed as the time went on.

"See here," he said once, "do let's put in some place for breakfast and a bath—" but the captain merely patted his shoulder, shook his head sadly and went on. "C'est la guerre."

"That's quite all right, of course," said Boppo, "but that's no reason why we should crawl around on our tummies without bathin', what? I mean to say, war or no, a chap's got to have a bath now and then, not?"

The captain sighed and patted Boppo's shoulder.

Eventually they came to Brière. The tiny market place was alive with humanity. Drawn up on the

Hôtel de Ville side were two regiments of infantry,
standing at ease and smoking nervously during the
temporary lull. Across from them—drawn up in front
of the market stalls—was a monstrous conglomeration
of carts piled high with household goods and a jab-
bering mob of refugees shrieking to high heaven in
excited French.

Boppo's detachment filed in and found a place to
squat down for a rest. For the nonce the captain
left them in Boppo's charge and went off to the
Hôtel de Ville. The girl and the two children simply
sat down with the detachment and looked steadily
at Boppo. Presently a buzz of new excitement filled
the tiny market square. Knots of refugees came over
to stare at the bedraggled remnants of Boppo's strong-
point garrison. The nearest soldiers stopped smoking
and pointed quite openly and rudely at Boppo and
his men and made an elaborate explanation to their
neighbors. Boppo was uncomfortable. Then presently
the girl shrieked in high falsetto and dragging the
two urchins at arms' length she streaked across the
square and hurled herself into the open arms of an
old man and an old woman.

Boppo blinked.

"Old home week, what?"

Then a frightful thing happened: A bugle blared
sharply and the two regiments of infantry stiffened
to rigid attention. The crowd of refugees fell back
in awe, and the staff captain, very flushed and vol-
uble, threaded through the square with the brigade
commander. They walked directly up to Boppo and
stopped while the captain finished his harangue. The
brigadier wiped at his watery eyes and then threw
back his shoulders. Smartly his hand whipped up

to the salute. Boppo ducked. The brigadier took his shoulders in both hands and drew Boppo to his breast in a sudden wave of emotion. Then slowly and solemnly he removed from his tunic the decoration of the Croix de Guerre and pinned it by its ribbon over Boppo's heart.

Boppo drew back in horror and stared at it—at the circle of faces—faces that pointed and cheered lustily.

"I say," he sputtered, "I say—you know—see here, and all that sort of thing." The soldiers were yelling now and throwing their képis into the air. Boppo sputtered on: "I say—some mistake, y' know, what? I'm not even *in* your jolly old army. Not *my* coat at all."

"It is the madness!" The captain and the brigadier sighed and shook their heads.

"Rot!" said George Stanley. "I think I jolly well ought to know. See here—some johnny pinched my bike yesterday—"

The captain and the brigadier made to embrace him again. He drew back sharply.

"None of that! Look here—I've a jolly good mind to report all this to my legation here. I've never even met you two chaps until this morning."

They sighed and shrugged.

"Mon pauvre brave!" said the brigadier, and two tears welled into his tired eyes.

"Nonsense," said Boppo. "Rot and silly nonsense. Need a bath, that's all—bath, shave and new bike. Stupid scene all this. No business to do it—to a perfect stranger too. Old enough to know better—both of you, what?" And he stalked off in high dudgeon. A sudden silence fell upon the market place as people drew back to let him through. Those nearest him shook their heads sadly.

Then suddenly out of the silence there came a shrill shriek. Boppo turned. Across the open space a girl with two children, an old man and an old woman were running after him as fast as they could.

"M'sieur Boppo!"

They were upon him before he could bolt, clinging to him—arms about his neck—sobbing and laughing and patting his hands.

"I *say*." He tried to draw back but they held to him. "I say—public street—hardly the thing, y' know. Do leave off, what? I mean to say, people will remark it, what?" But they clung to him, dragging him along with them—a chattering crowd of refugees in their wake. "Savior of our daughter's honor"—"protector of the innocent."

"Do stop it," said Boppo. But they kept on—shrieking it all backward in explanation to the people behind. "Noble soldier of Belgium." And presently they pushed him bodily through the doorway.

An hour later, bathed, dressed and shaven, Boppo sat down to his breakfast with the old woman on his right hand, the old man on his left, and the girl opposite—looking at him with starry eyes. Along the walls a motley array of aunts and cousins stood chattering and nodding in approval while Boppo ate. Then presently, as if by prearranged signal, they all filed gradually and solemnly out—leaving him alone with the girl. He looked at her uncomfortably. She lowered her eyes. He looked at the low ceiling. She looked at him again.

"Those your children?" he asked pleasantly by

ay of conversation. She blushed and shook her
ead violently. He looked at the table. She looked
t him. He looked at her. She looked at the table.
"Silly war," said Boppo. He looked at his finger
ails. She looked at him. He looked at her. She
lushed. He got up. She looked at him. He sat
own. He scratched his head absently with the middle
nger of his left hand.

"Stupid old general—this morning—what?"

She smiled and shook her head. He thought about
. for a moment and decided that he was vaguely
ncomfortable. He got up and walked to the door.
'he girl waited a moment and then followed him.
Ie looked out into the street.

"'Ullo," he said. *"Not* raining. Jolly, what?"

"You go, m'sieur?" There was a tremulous quaver
1 her voice.

"Well," Boppo hesitated. "Not now—shortly."

"Forever?"

"Oh, I say—beastly long time—forever, what?"

Then in the half light of the entry way she burst
1to tears and threw her arms about his neck.

He jumped backward, and his mouth fell open in
onsternation.

"I say," he said. "I say, y' know, and all that
ort of thing, what? That is, what I mean is—
ardly the thing."

But she clung to him more tightly. Then suddenly
e saw it over her shoulder.

"Ha!" he snorted. She drew back as he pointed
ito the street. "Look—silly ass who stole my bi-
ycle!" He pulled away from her and vaulted down
ie narrow steps to the pavé. The soldier trundling
ie bicycle stood suddenly still and saluted. Boppo

grabbed the handlebars and jerked them from the man's hands.

"Ha! Caught you. Ought to have you jolly well arrested, you silly ass!"

The soldier saluted again and marched stiffly away up the street. Boppo shouted after him:

"If you jolly well do it again, I shall!"

He put his leg over the bike and felt for the pedal. The girl touched his arm.

"You go now, m'sieur?"

"Absolutely," said Boppo. "Had jolly well enough—too much kissin'—not *my* war neither."

"And you never come back?"

"Not if I know m'self."

Again—furiously—she burst into tears and clung to him. He stood it miserably as long as he could, then he patted her shoulder. She looked up at him.

"See here—don't take it so badly," he sputtered. Then in a brilliant flash he removed the general's Croix de Guerre and pushed it into her hands.

"Keepsake—all that," he said awkwardly, and in the pause he pushed with his free foot and started pedaling down the street. After a moment he looked back. She was running after him as fast as she could. Then he got his second brilliant idea. He stopped and dismounted.

"See here," he shouted. "You can't come along y' know—*really*." He tapped his chest. "Me," he said, *wife!*" He traced in the air the outline of tremendous hips. "Wife," he repeated. "Wife and one, two, three"—he counted off seven fingers—*"children!"*

She stopped still in the middle of the street. For a moment they stared at each other. Then slowly

Boppo remounted his bicycle and pedaled off. At
the turn he looked back once more. She was stomp-
ing furiously upon something that lay upon the pavé—
something that glittered and writhed under her heavy
sabots as she pounded its fragility into muddy ob-
livion.

"Ha!" said Boppo. "Ha and what ho. Silly
women, silly soldiers," and after a moment, "wonder
what the stupid war was all about?"